JO JAMES

CHASING
SHADOWS

Complete and Unabridged

LINFORD
Leicester

First published in Great Britain in 2005

First Linford Edition
published 2006

British Library CIP Data

James, Jo
  Chasing shadows.—Large print ed.—
  Linford romance library
  1. Romantic suspense novels
  2. Large type books
  I. Title
  823.9'2 [F]

  ISBN 1–84617–492–9

Published by
F. A. Thorpe (Publishing)
Anstey, Leicestershire

Set by Words & Graphics Ltd.
Anstey, Leicestershire
Printed and bound in Great Britain by
T. J. International Ltd., Padstow, Cornwall

1

Dan Kingston had never felt a sense of belonging. As a child, he'd found his way into foster homes, one after the other. Everyone wanted to adopt babies, never older children from dysfunctional families. But finally a retired school teacher — he called her Aunty Alice — took him on. She paid to educate him at boarding school and university because, as she liked to say, 'This boy has potential.'

At thirty-two, he devoted his life to his successful Melbourne law practice. It became his substitute for belonging, but it didn't offer the emotional comfort he craved, and sometimes, such as today, he found his work grinding, repetitive. He stretched, strolled across to the window which looked out on the landscape of Melbourne. Below, people moved, ant-like from this height. He stretched again.

The phone rang.

The bright, distracting Kate Drewett came on the line.

'Dan, can you meet me for coffee, please?'

The tone of her plea triggered an alert signal in his head. She wanted something, but even knowing this, he agreed. Time with the rather head-strong young woman was exactly what he needed. The air around her always felt fresher, the conversation often on the edge of insane, but never dull.

When he arrived at the outdoor café close to his offices, she was already seated at a table. She had the widest brown eyes. If they didn't sparkle so much, she'd have looked permanently in a state of surprise. As she waved to him, he hoped she was as pleased to seem him as he was to see her.

As usual, she chatted madly, one thing after another. Her parents were fine, her brother, Greg, Dan's friend from university days, was in Sydney on business, Greg's kids were staying over

2

with her mum and dad. If he hadn't suspected her motives for wanting to see him earlier, he certainly did now. But he waited until the muffins and coffee arrived.

'Smells lovely, doesn't it?'

She held her cup with both hands, sniffing the aroma with her pert nose.

'So, to what do I owe the pleasure of this meeting, Ms Drewett?'

Her eyes assumed an innocence he distrusted.

'I wanted to see you.'

'Why?'

She stared back at him and pouted.

'Does there have to be a reason? I like being with you.'

'OK, and what else?'

She shrugged and put down her cup.

'It's the family. I love them all dearly, but it's a madhouse at home. You try working in that atmosphere.'

'But you managed to write your first book there.'

'Huh!' She shrugged. 'Can you believe it, Dad's taken up playing the clarinet again. Also, I can never get to the phone. Someone is always using it. Mum's letting Greg's kids run wild around the house. They buzz in and out of my room, muscle in on the computer. How on earth am I supposed to think creatively in that environment? It's hopeless.'

'Isn't it time you moved away from home anyway?'

He still hadn't worked out where the conversation was going.

'How can I afford a place of my own? Do you have any idea how hard it is to become a self-supporting writer in Australia?'

She dabbed a muffin crumb from her lips with her finger.

'There are empty shops all over the suburbs. You could lease one of those quite reasonably as an office.'

Her eyes lit up, almost glowed.

'It's funny you should say that.'

He'd been lured into her trap! He chewed on a portion of muffin and waited to hear how exactly.

'Your receptionist, Jill, told me you've got a spare back room you use to store your stationery. It's half empty, Dan. I could clean it out and turn it into a comfortable little nook. I'd stay out of your way, promise, and in return, I'll take care of your stationery needs, orders, stock reports, that kind of thing.'

He laughed at the very idea she'd keep track of everything, let alone the stationery, but the big question was, did he dare let her loose in his rather conservative practice?

'Please, Dan?'

Persuasive eyes pinned him down. He buckled under them.

'All right, but only until I take on another administrative assistant.'

'Ha, only a poor writer would be willing to work in a room the size of a closet.'

'You've seen it?'

Her voice sparkled.

'I already have a name for it — Writer's Cramp. Don't you love it?'

5

He couldn't hold back a smile.

'You didn't think to ask first and inspect later?'

'You don't mind, do you? Jill showed me.'

Obviously afraid he might rethink the idea, she stood up, planted a damp kiss on his cheek, and said, 'Thanks. OK if I storm the fort tomorrow?'

Kate moved in the next day, bringing her bubbly personality with her, announcing her arrival with, 'Hi, guys. I'm here.'

The staff leaped to assist her unload her computer and desk, and helped cram everything into the stationery room. Jill arranged a special afternoon tea, to welcome the distinguished mystery writer!

Dan looked to the heavens for solace. Life at the Kingston practice would never be the same. Already her vibrancy and her enthusiasm were distracting everyone. He promised himself he'd have a word with her tomorrow. On second thoughts, he decided he might have better luck if he spoke to his staff.

Kate soon settled into Writer's Cramp, hanging the name on the door, leaving it ajar. It attracted staff on their way to the tearoom, at the rear of the sixth floor, to pop in and ask how her book was going. Stephen Carstairs, Dan's junior partner, liked to linger, draping himself against the door jamb, looking down on her with condescending eyes. His floppy brown hair and round, baby face might pass as attractive, but not to Kate. She preferred the strong, silent type. Not that she'd had much experience with the opposite sex. She knew more about her fictitious characters than she did about the men around her. But Steve was hard to ignore.

He fancied himself as a writer, but mostly, he fancied himself. Still, she couldn't afford to offend him, for he was junior partner in the practice hierarchy. So she took time occasionally to discuss with him the stage she'd reached in her novel, and the problems she encountered.

Today, after he'd popped in to say, in his usual patronising tone, 'Keep up the good work, Kate,' she sat staring at her computer monitor.

He'd stalled her flow of ideas. Why wouldn't her lady detective, Fabian Farley, give her inspiration? When her phone rang, she picked it up quickly.

'Kate Drewett,' she said in her recently acquired successful writer's voice.

In contrast, the caller sounded jarringly crude.

'You're that detective woman, aren't ya?'

Wow, she thought, on the edge of her chair, what's this all about?

'No. I write detective novels. I'm Melbourne's Agatha Christie of the new millennium.'

Her lips twitched with a mischievous grin as she made her extravagant claim.

'Yeah, yeah.' His gravelly, impatient tone unsettled her. 'But I reckon ya're the best person to help me. I wanta confess to a crime.'

Kate's stomach muscles tightened.

She shifted the weight in her chair and asked in a mocking voice, 'You killed a cockroach?'

'If ya not gunna take this serious . . . '

A vision of her brother, Greg, flashed into her mind. Of course, the silly clown was having her on. He occasionally got a kick out of sending his kid sister up, especially since she'd sold her first novel. She decided to let him think he'd fooled her.

'I'm sorry I'm not qualified to hear confessions, but I can arrange for Father Casey to hear it.'

She grinned, delighted with her reply. This light-hearted interruption, as opposed to Steve's visit, could be just what she needed. But when the caller didn't laugh or respond in any way, uneasiness set in. In the silence, she could hear the caller breathing, not heavily, yet it spooked her into shrilling into the phone, 'I know it's you, Greg. Stop fooling around.'

'Greg? Got another boyfriend, have ya?'

The gravelly laugh brought an eruption of goose bumps. Of course, it wasn't Greg. He couldn't sound so mean. She slammed down the phone and, swishing back her ponytail, stalked across to Dan's office.

When she entered, he had his head bent over a pile of papers. Great hair, she thought — black, shiny, thick, curling slightly as it grazed his forehead and collar. In truth, he was her favourite person. If she were to write a profile of her ideal man . . . The thought made her uncomfortably warm. When he didn't look up, she coughed.

'A-hem.'

'If it's you, Katy, I'm busy. Come back later.'

His diary sat open. With a handy pencil she wrote her name into that day's box.

'You've forgotten our appointment.' Smiling, she pointed to the entry. 'It's right here.'

'Katy!' he growled without glancing up.

She clicked her fingers and said cheerfully, 'I guarantee what I have to say will be much more interesting than those dull old papers.'

She'd known Dan since her early teens. Greg had brought his friend from Melbourne University home for dinner eight or ten years ago, and that one night had turned into regular visits, for his only family, elderly Aunty Alice, had died.

'Mrs Drewett, your roast dinners are spectacular,' he'd told Kate's beaming mother on that first occasion.

After that he received the red-carpet treatment whenever he called. In her small female clique, Kate whispered of his dark good looks, his blue eyes. She used extravagant language to describe him, exaggerating a little about the way he looked at her, but not about the knot in her stomach when he glanced in her direction.

Alas, she realised later that the roast dinners were a blind. His reason for regular visits was to see her older sister,

Rosemary, who'd grown tall, leggy and beautiful. Katy tired of the opposite sex and transferred her energies to captaining the school basketball and swimming teams.

Rosie and Dan dated regularly, but to the family's surprise and disappointment, they split up. Her sister confided to her they'd agreed their relationship had no future. Dan was indifferent to her aspirations to be a model and to travel.

'I told you not to build up your hopes, Mum. They're too fond of themselves,' Kate confided to her mother. 'Believe me, the man's married to his work.'

Mrs Drewett had sighed.

'Oh, well, maybe he'll start noticing you. I could teach you how to roast a leg of lamb.'

'In your dreams, Mum. Who wants to be noticed by a roast-loving solicitor ten years my senior?'

Though he and Rosie were no longer an item, Dan continued to come for dinner once a week. Kate rationalised it had to be for her mother's home cooking. What other reason could there be?

A smile creased his bronzed complexion as he looked up with those unnerving blue eyes. She tried to stay tight-lipped, refusing to succumb to the smile which lit his face. He looked fabulous when he deigned to give you a glimpse of it.

Women fell for him. One searching look with those eyes of his and she'd witnessed it set the hearts of model-type females, who dropped into the office, phoned, sent e-mails, faxes, invited him for the weekend, a-flutter. Yet, somehow he retained his bachelor status.

He laid his pen on the desk, bringing her thoughts back to the moment.

'Are you still here?'

'Yes.'

'Then leave, Katy. Can't you see I'm busy?' he said with a good-natured smile.

'I wanted you to know I've had an odd phone call.'

She cleared some papers and propped on the near corner of his desk.

At last she had his attention. He leaned back in his expensive leather chair, steepled his fingers.

'What's so ground-breaking about that? Your life is full of odd people.'

She grinned. 'But they're writers. They invent their fantasies, they don't live them out.'

'And they're indolent, and I'm busy. Good morning, Kate.'

He dismissed her with a flourish of one hand.

'Our arrangement doesn't include me sorting out your personal problems.'

Before he could return his attention to his papers, she leaned forward.

'Honestly, Dan, I feel sure this wasn't a writer. He had a really mean voice and said he wanted to confess a crime.'

'Sounds like a writer bereft of ideas to me.'

Dan's words sounded sarcastic, but

his expression, hard and assessing, suggested she had his attention.

'He knew my name, that I was a writer, my phone number, and that's very odd, considering I've only recently got a line through to your offices.'

'After the publicity for your book, most of that information is out there. The phone number is curious, though. It suggests a hoax, one of your writer friends, perhaps, taking the mickey. If he rings again, tell him your solicitor will deal with him if he keeps pestering you. Now, back to Writer's Cramp.'

She eased off his desk and inched down her short skirt. Not that he'd ever been vaguely interested in anything physical about her, which was most discouraging. At twenty-two, a girl liked to think she had something which appealed to a man, even one who was conservative and thirty-two.

'Good idea, I'll tell him my solicitor has a potent right hook. That should fix it.'

He laughed.

'Better yet, don't answer the phone for an hour or two. I'm inclined to think the prankster has had his kicks. You'll probably never hear from him again. If you do, get the calls monitored.'

'You're right, I suppose.'

'Do I detect a note of disappointment? You'd like him to call back?' he enquired, frowning.

'Not exactly, but I'm always looking for new ideas for my next book and there are possibilities here.'

She was thinking, as she wandered from Dan's office, that getting ideas this way beat tossing and turning in bed at night, and long, dull hours of research in the stuffy atmosphere of the library, reading books on how to murder someone by poison.

Through the mists of her thoughts, she heard Dan call, 'Don't answer the phone. Get Jill to intercept any calls in the outer office.'

As Kate returned down the passage to Writer's Cramp, trying to decide whether to have her calls vetted at reception, the flat ring of her phone sounded. She quickened her pace, the lure of it too tantalising to resist. It wasn't until she reached to pick up the receiver that she hesitated, her hand poised. Dan had advised against it, and his advice was always worth considering. Hang it all, if it was one of her friends she might recognise the voice. She took a deep breath.

'Kate Drewett,' she said.

'Ah, Ms Drewett, having second thoughts about answering, was ya?'

The same harsh voice, the same intimidating tone. She sighed loudly into the phone.

'For goodness' sake, haven't you got something more interesting to do than pester me?'

'Look, lady, we're talking life and death here, and if you're as good a writer as the leaf on that book of yours, Not Without Guilt, reckons, ya won't hang up, y'll listen up real hard.'

Kate's body tensed, her dry mouth refused to speak as into the silence he drawled, 'No point in calling anyone, or having this traced. I'm in one of them public boxes. If ya don't say something now, I'll hang up and . . . '

'I thought you mentioned life and death,' she muttered, tracing her tongue over her lips. 'Why involve me?'

'You're a smart cookie. You can recognise a story when you hear it. I'm offering you the scoop of the year here. There's the basis of a real good yarn in what I've gotta say. Trust me, ya'd be a mug to hang up, and I don't think you are.'

Trust him? What a joke! And yet, she felt a nebulous kind of pleasure in his flattery. Besides, the words, material for a whole book, pressed her buttons. She could at least hear him out.

She said firmly, 'If you've really got something serious to confess, all I can offer is to come with you to the police.'

'No way. I can't involve the cops at this stage. And don't pretend you're not interested. I can hear it in yer voice.'

She forced herself back into her

make-shift office chair. The timber railings dug into her spine. It sounded 'way over the top, but there was no mistaking the determined edge to his tone.

He laughed throatily.

'Look, are ya going to meet me, or are ya too chicken?'

Chicken? Not Kate Drewett! She had a reputation for being adventurous, willing to try almost anything. Though it sounded a bit bizarre, perhaps even risky, it may disappoint and turn out to be a huge fizzer. Yet, the adrenalin of a challenge flowed freely through her veins, and she felt sorely tempted to accept this one.

'First, give me your name.'

'You don't need to know who I am. Just be parked by the wire fencing on the outskirts of the Northland Shopping Centre carpark down at the supermarket end by one thirty. I'll look out for that weary old car you drive. The writing business not paying well, eh?'

She drew in her breath. Was there anything he didn't know about her? It had to be someone she'd been in contact with.

'Here's the instructions, and ya'd better note them, so listen up, cos I'm only gonna say this once more. One thirty, the northern perimeter of the Northland carpark. Got that?' he rasped.

'Yes.'

Kate worked busily to tap it into her computer as he went on.

'Unlock the door of the front passenger seat at exactly one thirty, but don't open it, don't trouble yourself looking for me. I'll find you.'

'When? You didn't say when?'

'This arvo, of course.'

'Excuse me? This afternoon?'

'We're wasting time here. A woman's life depends on my swift actions. If ya don't show today, ya gonna be real sorry.'

The line went dead.

She sat immobile in her chair, her

fingers laced together, occupied, weighing up the pro
Yes, he'd spooked her a bit w
theatrical voice, and it very well c
be that friends from her writers' group
were pulling a fast one for the laughs.
But she couldn't deny the overwhelming
urge to uncover the identity of her caller,
and find out why he'd involved her.
Wouldn't every mystery writer who'd
earned her stripes want to?

How dare he challenge her and think
she wouldn't keep the appointment.

...her mind and con-

...e assignation information
...itor on to a notepad, a
kn... rtainty in her stomach, she
heard... vement. Quickly shoving the
note under some papers she shut down
the computer.

Dan stood at the door.

'How long have you been there?' she
demanded.

'Sorry if I frightened you. In the
middle of a crucial scene, were you?'

'Yes.'

Well, it had been a crucial scene
— on the phone.

'I thought I heard your phone ring. I
wondered if it was your prankster
again.'

Kate saw the cloud of concern in his
eyes. If she told him what she was
planning, he'd put all kinds of impedi-
ments in her way.

'Just a school friend inviting Jill and me to lunch.'

The white lies worried her, but even more, the glint in his eyes. Had he overheard part of her conversation? She dismissed the suspicion as an attack of pre-assignation butterflies.

'Is it OK if Jill goes off around a quarter to one?'

'Fine. Have a nice lunch.'

On his way out, Dan turned, gave the string holding the sign, 'Writer's Cramp', a twist, and smiled. His resident author was hiding something. Her warm dark eyes were hidden by an underbrush of secrecy. He'd only heard her say, 'One thirty,' into the phone, but her tone and the guilty start she'd given when she saw him standing at the door said a great deal more than any words. Added to that, she'd swished her ponytail over one shoulder, something he recognised as a gesture of uneasiness.

Kate Drewett was hatching another of her plots.

She had an impetuous streak which

he privately admired, but it gave him anxious moments. She was the nearest thing to a sister he'd ever have, and while she worked in his offices, he felt a need to protect her, in particular from herself. He glanced at his watch, just after twelve thirty. He put his head around the corner of his junior partner's office.

'Steve, I'm going out to stretch my legs for a while. Don't know how long I'll be away, but if anything urgent comes up, call me on the mobile.'

Steve nodded.

Dan went down to his car, stayed out of sight while he waited for Kate and Jill to leave, then followed them at a discreet distance. This was the only way to reassure himself Kate wasn't getting herself into something she couldn't handle.

Meanwhile, Kate outlined her plan to Jill as quickly as possible, then caught her friend's eyes with an intense gaze.

'Interested in spicing up your life?' she asked.

Jill shrugged.

'I don't think I've got the temperament to play sleuth. I'll probably get a twitchy nose or need to rush off to the loo.'

'But you're always so cool, so together. Besides, I need you. Come on, Jill, I'm talking adventure with a capital A.'

'What can I lose? I've cleared it with Dan. He thinks we're lunching with a mutual friend.'

Kate laughed, excited now the assignation with Mr X was going ahead.

'In case something goes wrong, we'd better leave a note telling the boss where we really are,' Jill suggested.

'Of course. I'll handle it.'

Jill's comment had sown seeds of doubt in Kate's mind, but how could she give up the chance of meeting the guy who'd put out a challenge to her, and hopefully she'd pick up ideas for her novel? It took around forty minutes for her to reach the vast Northland shopping complex. As arranged, she parked outside the Wood Street entrance until Jill had time to drive in from Murray Road and position herself in a parking bay shadowed by the grey walls of the supermarket.

Kate searched for Jill's hatchback as she motored slowly towards the arranged spot, a healthy walk from the shops. It was eerily quiet, for few people parked this distance from the centre except in peak periods. She spotted Jill's car and pulled into a bay which fitted Mr X's instructions but also favoured a position from where Jill could observe without being noticed.

Turning off the engine, she took several deep breaths. Her car clock told her she had one more minute to wait. Goose bumps erupted over her body as she scanned the lonely landscape through her rear vision mirror. Nothing. If someone had been stringing her along, she'd be desperately disappointed.

Her shoulders ached from sitting so stiffly, trying to regulate her breathing.

Was he somewhere out there, waiting? The time moved on to exactly one thirty. Holding her breath, she reached across and unlocked the passenger front door. The roar of a motorcycle pounded as she turned to watch it disappear behind her. The engine cut out, she returned her gaze to the rear vision mirror, and suddenly the image of a man darkened it. This did not have the feel of a practical joke.

With slow, deliberate steps the motorcyclist approached her car.

Concentrate, she urged herself, study and mentally record everything about him. Early forties? Uncertain, because he walked with a slight stoop, but certainly crumpled, stained jeans, a red check flannel shirt under a leather jacket matched the rough voice of her caller.

The bike helmet gave him a disturbing, space invader appearance, but a bunch of keys dangling from his belt placed him of this world. Without taking her eyes from the mirror, she reached down and triggered the tape recorder she'd secured earlier to her vehicle's floor.

He stood by the open car door. She shifted in her seat, sweating as he removed his leather gloves. As he slapped them into his palm, she flinched, but only once, before straightening her back. He was trying to intimidate her, but he wouldn't win. As he folded himself into the seat beside her, she observed grubby trainers, smelled cigarette smoke and cleared her throat.

'Aren't you going to remove your hat as a gentleman would, Mr . . . er . . . ?' she said, attempting to sound cool, unfazed, but her crackly voice let her down.

'Did I claim to be a gent?'

His mean-spirited laugh confirmed him as her unknown caller.

'I wouldn't have believed you, anyway,' she said and sounded calmer, congratulating herself on her control. 'Did you give me your name?'

'You can call me Tom, luv.' She almost giggled nervously.

'How surprising. Jones or Smith?' she asked cynically.

'Tom Jones, naturally,' he mocked.

In case he could hear her wild heartbeat in the brief silence which followed, she hurried on.

'Mr Tom Jones, I can only spare five minutes. Why am I here?'

'Five minutes is all I need. I take it you know what a hitman is.'

'I'm a crime writer. Of course I do — a paid assassin.'

'Well, I'm one.'

Kate dragged in her breath, stared at him. Was she really sitting next to a hitman? Instinct told her he was making this up.

'Oh, come on, spare me the theatrics. I don't believe you, so if you're trying to scare me, Mr Jones, it's not working. Frankly, you look more like a man down on his luck to me.'

'Sorry, sister, but I'm a hitman, and if you're gonna keep interrupting me . . .'

The tape recorder whirred like an egg whisk into the momentary stillness, so she raised her voice.

'OK, I'm listening.'

She straightened up in her seat and risked a nervous peep in the wing mirror to check Jill was still around, and blinked. Surely that wasn't Dan's dark blue car parked near Jill's car! Of course not. There were plenty like it around.

'You got someone out there watching us by any chance?'

His unpleasant voice regained Kate's attention in a rush. She forced a laugh.

'Of course not.'

He had to believe she'd come alone. Suppose he really was a hitman? It didn't bear thinking. A second thought disturbed her even more. She may have dragged Jill into something unsavoury. Dan would be furious.

'You promised me a story and that's the only reason I'm here, but I have to say, so far it's shaping up as a waste of my time. If you'd take that stupid helmet off, it might give you some credibility.'

So there, she thought, pleased with the way she seemed to be controlling the conversation. The man wasn't at all scary, really, probably a crank with too much time on his hands.

'If you're genuinely worried about this confession, as you claimed earlier, wouldn't it be more sensible to go to the police than involve me?'

'You call yourself a writer? I'd 'ave thought that was bleeding obvious. You reckon the cops u'd believe a hitman? Besides, a bloke'd be dead before he reached there. I want you to tell the cops. Now, here's the drill, so listen up.'

Her stomach clenched and she took a deep breath.

'OK,' she said and waited.

* * *

It was close to two thirty when Kate pulled her car into the small carpark reserved for Dan's employees at the rear of their offices. She couldn't wait to get into Writer's Cramp and play the tape. Had she got all their conversation? Did she get any of it? But her anticipation flagged when she spotted Jill's car. Jill was supposed to follow Mr Tom Jones!

She slipped the tape recorder into her shoulder bag and on shaky legs made her way into the offices. Jill was sitting at the reception desk, looking unusually flustered and raised her eyebrows as if apologising when she saw Kate.

'So why didn't you follow him?' Kate asked in a demanding undertone.

Jill leaned towards her and whispered, 'You'll never guess. Dan arrived and recognised my car, and yours.'

'How did he find us at Northland?'

'You're far too obvious. I bet he suspected you were up to something. He followed us, of course.'

Kate gave a long sigh. Her temperature began to rise.

'And I suppose he prevented you from following my man in the motorbike helmet?'

'Actually, he ordered me back to the

office. Kate, what else could I do? I need my job.'

Kate touched her arm.

'It's my fault. I had no right to drag you into it. I'll speak to Dan. Eat humble pie and ask for his forgiveness. So where is your illustrious boss now? Waiting in his office to tick me off, I suppose.'

'No. He hasn't come back. He probably stopped off for a late lunch.'

Kate folded her arms, leaned close and whispered conspiratorially, 'Did you have an opportunity to view Jonesy?'

She waited for Jill's answer, butterflies in her stomach.

'Who?'

'Our man. He says his name's Tom Jones, ha ha.'

Jill giggled.

'I got an excellent view of his body through the binoculars and drew a few conclusions. He's definitely not centrefold material. To be honest he looked down and out, homeless, maybe? Did he ask for a loan? I'm dying to know what he said.'

The phone rang. Jill picked up the receiver, covering the speaker with her hand.

'I guess I'll have to hold on a bit longer.'

Kate eased herself from the desk.

'It's a lot more intriguing than you think. Can you stay on tonight? We'll listen to the tape together. Oh, and don't mention it to anyone, will you?'

'So long as Dan doesn't ask me why I'm staying back.'

'Be a bit inventive. Say we're planning a surprise party. It's the truth — a surprise party for Jonesy.'

Kate laughed uneasily as she strolled towards Dan's office. There, she flopped into his expensive swivel chair and did a couple of spins. She was on her way around for a third time, rehearsing the speech she'd deliver to him, when she heard him stride up the passage. He arrived as she straightened up to face him. He looked vaguely hassled.

She tapped her fingers firmly on the desk and stared up at him with tight lips. His wide grin rather threw her.

'You followed me,' she accused.

'Out of my chair, Ms Drewett.'

He crossed to the back of the desk, unsettling her with his lawyer's courtroom voice. She stood immediately, and Dan dropped into his chair. It felt warm. Kate had left behind a perfume, a delicate fragrance of flowers. Every now and then she sent him these physical reminders of her growing beauty and attractiveness. Unfortunately, though, the growing up for her didn't include a sense of responsibility. Today's escapade was another example of that.

She'd always had appealing eyes which either shone with exuberance or mischief. Now there was something else in their depths. She'd also stopped dressing in long, loose skirts, socks and boots, like a writer who hadn't yet made it. Perhaps her publishers had suggested the change as more appropriate for promotional book signings, but she now even had an air of sophistication that was extremely eye-catching.

'You didn't say why you followed me.'

Her eyes glowered with suspicion. He shrugged, deliberately unresponsive, hoping she'd be lured into saying more than she intended.

'You usually shop out at Northland, do you?' she enquired.

'It depends on what I'm looking for. What were you buying out there, Kate?'

She slid off his desk with an impatient movement.

'You know why I was there, and you muddied all my plans by showing up and ordering Jill back to the office.'

He eased forward.

'I didn't know, but I did suspect you were up to something, and I was right. I followed you because I wanted to protect a valuable member of my staff. You knew I've never approve of involving Jill in your foolhardy plans, yet you went right ahead and did it.'

Kate's cheeks turned pink. She ran

an index finger down one.

'She's the coolest person I know.'

He pushed a folder to one side and rested his elbows on the arms of the chair.

'She may be, but that doesn't give you the right to ask her to follow a crazy lead because there may be a storyline in it for you. It's thoughtless and inexcusable.'

'I'm really sorry, Dan. I didn't put her at risk. I asked her because I needed some back-up. You won't blame her, will you? I did rather twist her arm.'

'If you had to go, why not ask me?'

'Oh, sure, you'd have leaped at it, wouldn't you? I went because I don't like people using me for some mysterious reason. I thought I was entitled to at least investigate the man's claims, and, thanks to you, I have no idea who Jonesy is now,' she wailed, waving her hands.

'He gave you a name? What else did he say?'

'Not much.'

Her lip drooped petulantly. She examined her fingernails. She was misleading him again, giving him only part of the story.

'Out with it. What did he actually say?' Dan insisted.

'It's all buzzing around in my head. I'll go put it into the computer, put my thoughts in some kind of order and get back to you later.'

A ray of sunshine caught the gold of her hair, the deep, luminous brown of her eyes. She looked incredibly vulnerable and his resolve to be tough on her disappeared like a flash.

He found himself saying, 'Don't you want to know what I did after you left the Northland carpark?'

'You mean you . . . '

'I might have.'

'Stop teasing me, Dan Kingston. What aren't you telling me?'

'I followed your mystery caller.'

She covered her mouth with her hand as if to stop it flying open.

'Lost for words? That has to be a

first.' Dan couldn't disguise the amusement in his voice.

'You followed him?'

'I couldn't disappoint you, could I?'

She ran to his side and planted a kiss on his cheek.

'Oh, Dan, you're wonderful. Quickly, tell me what happened.'

She was back on the edge of the desk, leaning forward, her eyes shining in anticipation.

'What was he driving? Where did he go?'

He grinned.

'One question at a time. He rode the same bike from Northland, and I followed him to the Imperial Hotel in Northcote.'

Her eyes widened.

'And? Is he staying there? What name is he using? Come on, Dan, this is like drawing teeth.'

He left his seat and walked across to the window. Hands in his trouser pockets, he turned back, feeling rather foolish.

'Actually, I lost him.'

3

Kate groaned. 'How could you?' she asked, desperate to know what had gone wrong.

'He went into the pub but didn't come out.'

She clapped the palm of one hand to her head.

'Men! It didn't occur to you to follow him in, keep him under surveillance?'

He strolled across to the half-open door and closed it.

'Stop interrupting.' His voice hardened. 'So you want to hear the rest?'

'I'm listening. I'm listening.'

'Your nasty caller left his bike outside the hotel. My guess is he expected to be followed and used the pub as a place to pass through and leave by the back entrance.'

It made sense, but she snapped.

'Did you think to get the registration

number? And what happened to the motorbike? If it's still there, he might go back for it. I could take a quick run out for a look-see.'

'Yes, I got the registration number, but after the man disappeared into the hotel, a shapely blonde, wearing leather jacket and pants, with an absurdly obvious sway came out and took off on the bike.'

Kate drew in her breath.

'It must have been him in disguise. You followed him?'

'It wasn't him, not with those slinky hips, but I did follow her to another pub in Fitzroy. Same thing happened. She went into the building. Ten minutes later another man came out and took off on the bike. That's when I decided I was being given the run-around and came back to the office.'

Kate groaned.

'You wimped out? I'd have kept on the scent.'

'In case it's escaped your notice, I run a law firm. Now we've done all we can, I want your promise you'll go to the police, or forget it. If you're not using these premises to write then you'll have to vacate the room.'

Kate certainly didn't want to lose her little nook, but Dan didn't sound over-fussed.

'You're far too nice a guy to do that. Can I have the registration number?'

Dan retuned to his chair.

'Since I did the chase, I'm following it up, and don't depend on me being Mr Nice Guy. Push me too hard and you're out.'

Pouting, she hurried to the door, for once erring on the side of good sense. Back in Writer's Cramp, she wondered if she'd banked too heavily on the warm relationship she had with Dan. If she decided to pursue Jonesy, she'd have to avoid upsetting Dan and that included the arrangement she'd made with Jill to listen to the tape tonight.

Unable to concentrate on her novel, her mind constantly strayed back to the audio tape. It was too early to tell Dan she'd risked making the recording, so she listened to it only once, muffling the sounds with her jumper, pressing her ear to the woollen parcel. At least she was able to confirm she had quite a slice of their conversation. When she replayed it later, she expected to learn a lot more about Jonesy. She glanced at her watch, picked up the phone and keyed in Jill's number.

'OK for six o'clock?'

Jill lowered her voice into the receiver.

'Did you square things with Dan?'

'He doesn't blame you. He knows how persuasive I can be.'

'OK, it's in my own time, so I'll be there. Don't start without me.'

'Roll on six o'clock.'

Kate put down the phone then headed for Dan's office.

'I'm staying back tonight, so I'm slipping out for a sandwich.'

He glanced up.

'Can you get me a roast beef sandwich, please? Ask Angelo to put it on my tab. I'll fix him when I'm in there next.'

When Kate returned, she dropped his sandwich on his desk without disturbing him and spent the remaining hour or so consigning to the computer as much as she could recall of the details of Jonesy's original phone conversations, her encounter with him in the car, his appearance, her impressions, her ideas, her questions.

At last, a knock signalled Jill's arrival.

As she swung the door open her friend whispered, 'So what did Jonesy have to say? How did the tape turn out? I'm dying to hear it.'

Kate locked the door, cleared the floor and, sitting down, opened a brown paper bag containing the sandwiches she'd bought earlier.

'Help yourself,' she said.

Jill joined her on the floor, making herself comfortable with her back against a wall.

'You expect me to eat when I'm hanging out for the old rocker's story?'

'You know, the more I think about it, the more I think the guy's story is so unlikely it could be true.'

'What could be true? What did he say?'

'Basically, he told me he was a hitman, hired to kill a woman called Helen Porter and he wants me to tell the police.'

'You're kidding me!' Jill shrieked.

'Shush. Dan might hear us. Jonesy claims he accepted an assignment to kill a person named Helen Porter.'

'It's crazy.'

'It's all on the tape.'

Kate reached into her drawer, retrieved the recorder and tape and set it up.

'I'll have to keep the sound down. We'll listen first and talk later.'

Throughout the scratchy tape, every now and then the sound of Kate drawing in her breath came through.

'He spooked you, didn't he?' Jill said at the end.

'No, he astounded me with his claims.'

'It still doesn't make any sense to me.'

'He reckons one day while he was tailing this Helen Porter, looking for an opportunity and a method to snuff out her lights, he followed her into a supermarket, and found himself standing behind her at the checkout. Apparently, she struck up a conversation with him about her children.'

'I suppose that could be true, but it's rather far-fetched.'

Kate bit into her sandwich, but hardly tasted it as she thought aloud.

'As Jonesy put it, the woman was a looker, nice, a good sort with soft blue eyes like his ma's. He knew then he couldn't go through with it, but because he's a known criminal and wants to remain anonymous, he can't go to the police and report a contract is out on this woman. That's where I come in. He wants me to inform them the woman's life is in danger.'

'You can't tell me a man like that would recognise decency or soft blue eyes, let alone equate them with his mother. Do you know what I think, Kate?'

'Tell me.'

'He's a frustrated novelist and this yarn about hitmen and warm eyes is in one of his manuscripts. He wants your attention and he hopes this will persuade you to read his work. Before you know it, you'll have a manuscript on your doorstep. He'll be back to you any time now.'

'But why me? Why not some really well-known writer?'

'Because they'd be too busy, too cynical. You're new to the industry. You know how desperate people can get to have an editor read their work.'

Kate laughed, folding her knees to her chest.

'Tell me about it, but I've never been that desperate. Let's get back to what he said. The contract to kill came through an intermediary but he's fairly certain it was put out by a former boyfriend of Porter's.'

'It's usually the husband who murders the wife in books, isn't it?'

'Actually, in real life, it's nearly always the husband, too. You heard Jonesy say that he expects someone else will take it when he refuses the job. So where do I go from here?'

'Play the tape again. We could have missed something,' Jill said.

Kate had her finger on the rewind button when a knock, followed by the rattle of the door handle startled them. Jill sprang to her feet, looked around her, but there was nowhere to hide, no cupboard to creep behind.

The door rattled again.

Dan called, 'Kate, I asked for a roast beef sandwich. This one is cheese and tomato.'

Kate put her finger to her lips.

'Hide somewhere,' she hissed.

Jill gestured the impossibility of her request with raised hands and shoulders as Kate stuffed the tape recorder back into the drawer. Taking a deep breath, she unlocked and opened the door slightly.

'Dan,' she said, forcing a smile, 'sorry, we've eaten your sandwich.'

Jill, who now stood behind her, jabbed her in the ribs, which added to Kate's discomfort, but somehow she held her nerve. Dan's glance swept across to Jill. He frowned.

'OK which one of you is going to explain what you're doing? Jill?'

'We were listening to the . . . ' Jill began.

Kate chipped in before she could give anything away.

'Dan, it's got nothing to do with you, or your firm. We're on our own time.'

'Jill?' he prompted.

Kate exaggerated a sigh of frustration.

'If you insist, but you're a real party pooper. We wanted it to be a surprise. Now you've spoiled everything. We were planning an office party for your birthday.'

'It's not for months,' he growled.

'We're planning ahead, so please leave us to get on with it.'

'And if I don't want a surprise party?'

'You're not getting a surprise party now that you've killed that idea. But we'll keep you informed of our change of plans.'

She put her weight on the door. He stepped back, withdrawing a little too easily for her peace of mind. Still, when she finally had the door closed and Dan outside, she released a long breath.

'How did you find the bottle to give him all that guff about the party?' Jill asked.

'It was our contingency plan, wasn't it? I simply changed it from being a party to his party. Have you forgotten I'm a writer?' Kate smiled, before turning serious. 'But don't think for a minute we've fooled him. He knows that's not what we're doing. He's retired to let us simmer. Since he's out of the way for the time being, we may as well proceed. Tomorrow will take care of itself.'

'Heavens, I can't afford to lose my job. I'm backing off, Kate. I want out.'

'Dan won't sack you. You know everything that happens in this practice. You're too valuable.'

'Kate, you're doing it again, not listening to me.'

Jill shivered.

'What's the matter? You look cold,' Kate asked.

'It just occurred to me. If this Jonesy is right, someone else will murder the Porter woman. There are people around who'll do anything for money. Go to the police as Jonesy asked, Kate. Give them the tape and let them deal with it.'

'I'm a writer. They'd say it's a practical joke. I want more evidence before I go to them. I'm going to try to find out if this Helen Porter exists.'

Kate arrived at the office early next morning having decided, during a sleepless night, that the sensible thing to do was to confide in Dan. She found him in the tearoom.

'Just the man I wanted to see,' she said lightly.

'I thought you'd be avoiding me after

I caught you out last night.'

'Why can't you trust me?'

'That's like asking a bird to trust a hungry little kitten.'

She laughed.

'You're a legal eagle, not an ordinary bird. Surely you're not afraid to trust a little pussy cat like me?'

'When I'm dealing with someone who possesses a persuasive purr and an inventive mind, I feel uncomfortably helpless.'

He turned away, his face crinkling with a grin.

'My office. You have some explaining to do.'

She blew a strand of hair from her face, assured herself she'd weathered one more crisis, and followed him along to his office.

'Close the door, please.'

She raised her brows, closed it, and as usual, parked herself on the corner of his desk and waited.

'Yesterday, I disturbed you and Jill discussing that impostor you met.

Don't bother to deny it. What little plans did you hatch?'

His tone wasn't accusing, rather interested, so, confident she'd never get a better opportunity, she produced the tape from her handbag and held it up.

'This is what we were discussing. I taped my conversation with Jonesy.'

'You what?'

'I hid a recorder under my seat in the car. That's what detectives do, isn't it?'

'Katy, Katy, what am I going to do with you? You could have . . . '

She put her fingers to her lips to indicate silence.

'It's OK, Dan. I'm still in one piece. Would you like to hear it?'

She inserted the tape into her recorder, set it on the desk and switched it to play.

Dan leaned back in his chair, thinking, assessing, trying to analyse what he heard as he listened to the scratchy record of Kate's meeting with Jonesy.

'Well,' she said, when it had finished,

'what do you think?'

Too often Kate tested his patience with her lack of judgment. She'd always been the same, only he'd noticed that the risk-taking seemed to accelerate as she grew older. He leaned forward in his chair.

'This only reinforces my earlier opinion.'

He removed the tape, held it towards her.

'If the guy is for real and knows you have this, he'll want it. It could incriminate him. Things have gone beyond a nutter having a good time on the phone with an attractive young lady. He asks you to go to the police. Do it.'

4

Kate reached over for the tape, but Dan kept his fingers firmly locked around it.

'And tell them what?' she said, her bottom lip jutting petulantly.

'That this bloke rang you, you foolishly agreed to meet him and after that, I suggest you let the tape tell the rest of the story.'

'You're the one with the law degree. You know they wouldn't act on flimsy evidence like that. They'd joke about me being a mystery writer and having a vivid imagination, and then condescendingly agree to look into it. And it's guaranteed I'd never hear from them again. The very fact that I am a mystery writer tells me that's exactly what would happen.'

'This isn't a rattling good yarn you've walked into. And you're not a detective. Give the police the tape, Kate.'

'I really wish that once in a while you could break free from your bowler hat and umbrella bonds and do something really exciting. You spend your life protecting people's rights, listening to their complaints. Don't you ever get the bug to be out there checking up on their stories, not waiting for one of your lackeys to get the goods on them? Don't you ever want to know for sure if they're guilty or not guilty?'

He'd always thought of his work as rewarding, sometimes challenging and interesting, sometimes repetitive, never exciting enough to make him glow, as Kate did now.

'I'm upholding the law. That's my job, and it's a noble profession.'

He slid back into his chair, regretting his defensive reply, disliking these periods when he felt uncertain, vaguely drifting.

'It sounds so stuffy. Can't I tempt you to do one more investigative job with me before we hand on the tape? It would be fun. Blow away the old cobwebs.'

There were moments of madness, too often lately, when all his training, all his commonsense deserted him and he found himself vulnerable to Kate's powers of persuasion.

'By getting mixed up with a hired gun?' he said, while inside, a voice of restlessness urged him to do just that.

'I can't put my finger on it, but there's something on that tape that we're missing.'

She paused, mentally keying her thoughts back to the taped conversation.

'We know Jonesy exists. He actually sat next to me, spoke to me. Yet I have this sense he wasn't there. He was a ghost. It's occurred to me how well-rehearsed his story sounded. One thing's for sure. He reeked of smoke, and had a bundle of keys attached to his jeans. Fact, he smokes, possibly he rehearsed his lines, certainly uneducated.'

She linked her fingers. They were long with trimmed, unpainted nails, unsophisticated, as she was, different from her sister.

'If only I'd seen his eyes. Eyes can say so much about a person,' she added. 'Hey, that's triggered another memory. How could I have forgotten? When I turned my head to get a better look at Jonesy, I noticed he wears a pony tail. It had escaped from under his helmet.'

'Think, Kate, think, something else might come to mind.'

She chewed on her lip but shook her head.

'So, we're looking for a smoker who wears a red check shirt, a pony tail, a bunch of keys attached to blue jeans, rides a motorbike, which reminds me, I have the registration number. I'll do some checking on that today. Any tattoos?'

'I only saw his hands. Everything else was covered.'

'So how would your Mrs Farley proceed from here?'

'First, she'd try to find the house where Jonesy's supposed victim lives. It shouldn't be hard. He gave a very good description of it on the tape. And, my new deputy has agreed to trace the owner of the bike.'

'Will do,' he agreed.

She slid off his desk, straightened her skirt.

'There, you see, you're as keen as I am to get to the truth. So we're a team?'

He shrugged. If he got her on his side, he might be able to convince her to keep him informed. That way, very little harm could come to her.

'I'm giving you one more day.'

'Forty-eight hours,' she bargained.

'Take it or leave it — twenty-four.'

'OK.'

She came to his side, looked down at him with glowing eyes, and, as usual when he pleased her, she dropped a sisterly kiss on to his cheek. But this time, he had to fist his hands together, struggle with an impulse to reach out, to hold her and tell her he couldn't bear it if anything happened to her.

She leaned forward again.

'Hey, what's this?'

He felt the soft pad of one finger ripple through his hair.

'I do believe, a grey hair,' she piped, as if she'd discovered gold.

'Only one? I'm surprised my hair didn't turn grey overnight after you moved in.'

'I wouldn't worry. A touch of grey can add to an older man's charisma, make him look more distinguished. You're still the best-looking male around here,' she teased.

He wheeled his chair away from his desk.

'Enough of this nonsense, and scat. Go find out if a Mrs Porter exists, where she lives and where she goes shopping. But do it discreetly. Remember, if we're partners, you must promise not to go off on your own, without first consulting me. Bargain?'

'Huh! I'm doing all the leg work.'

'And loving it. If you find out Porter and Smith exist then I can do a background search on them.'

'It's Jones, not Smith. Can I have the

tape back? I want to listen to it again. There's something buzzing around in my head, something I'm missing.'

'Fine, but it goes into the safe before you leave here today.'

'I take it I can call on Jill for some help?'

Kate made towards the door. He guessed she planned to escape before she heard him refuse. He strode to her side, swung her gently around.

'Definitely not. She's paid to look after this business. I will not have her attention diverted by your madcap schemes.'

She smiled and looked down at his hand which still rested on her arm.

'She'll be very disappointed.'

'I'll deal with Jill. You get on with your snooping. Your time's running out.'

He watched her stroll off down the passageway leaving him with an image of a satisfied grin on her lips, and a curious feeling, both arousing and puzzling, that the girl had very definitely become a woman — a woman who always managed to outsmart him.

At her door, she turned, saw him still standing there, and called, 'Jill thought the bit on the tape about Jonesy thinking Helen had eyes like his mother was bunkum. Do you agree?'

'Unbelievable,' he replied, unnerved by the realisation that he was referring to Kate, not Helen Porter.

Kate locked herself in her office, replayed the tape, and printed out the computer notes she'd made earlier about Jonesy. She studied the information several times before casting it aside in disgust, unable to discover what it was that troubled her about them.

Time to see if Helen Porter really existed, she decided. If she did, as Jill pointed out earlier, the woman could be in danger. She had Jonesy's description of the Porter home and the district, also the information that the woman drove her children to school every day via a St George's Road. She reached for the street directory.

On her way out, she confided in Jill behind her hand.

'Just going out to find Helen Porter's house. I've cleared it with Dan.'

'Don't forget to don your moustache and glasses.' Jill laughed.

'Aren't you going to wish me luck?'

'You won't need it. You were born lucky.'

* * *

Kate turned the car into St George's Road and then into another of the small streets off it. The traffic had been very heavy, but it had grown quiet in this small residential area. This was the last avenue, and there it was. Excitement and anticipation coursed through her.

Number Eight was exactly as Jonesy had described it, impressively contemporary. It managed to look ugly amidst the magnificence of traditional mansions of an earlier century. Its fence line of pencil pines was yet to reach its grand potential so that the pebbled driveway which swept up to paved steps leading to the glazed entrance was clearly visible.

Kate let out a long breath. Had she found Helen Porter? Then she saw a **For Sale** notice erected on the lawn of the house next door. She stared at it, ideas stirring in her imagination, but for now she had to decide whether to chance it and go into the Porter home hoping to meet Helen Porter, maybe warn her.

She parked her car beneath the shadows of an old plane tree several houses away, and waited, hoping something might happen. Into the stillness came the soft hum of an expensive engine, the crush of tyres against pebbles. A car swung out of Number Eight's drive and she bobbed down out of sight. As it sped off, hang it all, she missed the number plate, but clearly noted the driver was male.

Her heart racing, she decided to take a chance. After adjusting her rear view vision mirror, she slipped a hand through her hair and released her pony tail. Her hair bounced around her face, but she still looked like Kate Drewett.

She applied a heavy layer of make-up. Blushing cheeks and a pink mouth smiled back at her. If only she'd thought to bring a pair of spectacles.

She recalled a towel in the back seat. Aha, she thought, as she loosened her shirt from her trousers, and stuffed the towel up it. If Jonesy lay somewhere in wait, watching her movements, he wouldn't recognise a pregnant woman. Ideas flashed through her mind, so did Dan's warning. But he'd agreed to her trying to establish Helen Porter's existence and there was a simple way to do this. The woman was the key to her finding answers to the Jonesy affair.

Stepping on to the pavement, sweat trickled down her back as her shoes crunched the tiny pebbles beneath her feet on the driveway. The towel against her stomach seriously threatened to dislodge. Adrenalin surged through her as she pressed the door button. It took only seconds before she heard the sound of high heels tapping on the floor. She adjusted the towel, dampened her lips with the tip of her tongue as the door swung open.

The woman was tallish, with well-trained blonde hair curved about her face. Mid-thirties, Kate thought, beautiful, if you admired cool eyes, together looks and superior smiles.

'Yes?' she said in a posh voice, her aloof eyes pausing at Kate's bump.

Kate forced out the words.

'I'm Paula Hastings.' She held out her free hand. 'Mrs Porter?'

The woman ignored it. 'Excuse me?'

Kate placed her briefcase on the white-tiled porch and opened her Filofax.

'You are Mrs Helen Porter?'

'Porter's my business name, and you are?'

'I'm here to reprogramme your computer,' she invented.

'It's at the office. There's been a mix-up with my business premises and here.'

'It's your business? I thought your husband . . . '

Kate knew instantly that her question had come too quickly. In her anxiety, she'd overlooked the need for a detective's finesse.

'My husband runs the firm. Leave your business card. I'll tell him you called.'

Her business card read, **Kate Drewett, author**. Her stomach doing hand turns, said the first thing which came to mind.

'I recently joined the company. My business cards haven't been printed yet.'

Even Helen Porter's sigh managed to sound superior.

'I'm surprised they'd take on a woman in your condition.'

'Pardon me?' Kate said.

The woman's gaze lingered on her stomach.

'Oh, you're referring to my pregnancy? There are laws about discriminating against . . . '

Porter gave her a withering stare as she began closing the door.

'I'd be happy to call at your business

premises. I can make it this evening. The address is . . . ?' Kate managed to say.

'Good evening, Ms Hastings.'

The door closed, and a chill swept over Kate. The woman sounded suspicious. She quelled the inclination to race down the driveway and escape into her car by forcing herself to take deliberate steps.

Driving home, her head spun as she tried to interlock the few pieces she had of the puzzle. She couldn't wait to discuss them with Dan. He'd be cross, but she could convince him she couldn't pass up the opportunity to see if Helen Porter was home. As she pulled into her street, she noticed Dan's car parked outside the house. He'd come to see her, she thought, pleasure rippling through her.

He was in the sitting-room, talking to her dad when she entered. They both looked up as she came into the room.

'What have you been up to now, love?' her father asked.

She shook her head.

'Nothing important.'

It sounded guilty. Her face felt hot.

'So what's with the padding around your stomach? Playing Santa in drag are you?' Dan asked, grinning.

Her father laughed. 'Who'd know what our Kate's planning next?'

Kate tried to laugh with them. How could she have forgotten the padding!

'I was experimenting for my latest novel. Fabian, my private sleuth, pretends she's pregnant. I wanted to see if it works. And it does. I fooled the woman I just called on. I'll fill you in tomorrow, Dan. Catch you later, Pops.'

She hurried to her bedroom, but a thought sent her back to the sitting-room in quick time.

'What brings you here, Dan?'

'I'm taking Rosemary to a concert.'

'Oh, you didn't mention it earlier.'

She couldn't keep the disappointment from her voice. Rosemary stepped into the room, smelling irresistible, looking irresistible and claimed the limelight. Dan looked such a dreamboat in his formal gear, Kate had the strangest wish that given one wish she'd choose to swap places with Rosie for the night.

'Excuse me for a minute, Rosemary,' she heard him say. 'I need to speak to Kate.'

He led her into the hallway.

'You've been to the Porter house, haven't you?'

'I might have.'

'Yes or no?' he insisted, sounding slightly irritated.

'You won't believe what I found out.'

'Dan, we're going to be late,' Rosemary called, and her high heels tapped in their direction.

'You have an appointment in my office first thing tomorrow, Kate. We can discuss the matter then.'

★ ★ ★

Dan arrived at his office early. This confounded thing with Katy was eating into his time, putting him behind with his schedules. He should have insisted she go to the police at the beginning. He sighed as he listened for her arrival, damning himself for allowing a bright young woman with eager, luminous eyes and the enthusiasm of a schoolboy riding a rocket bound for outer space to involve him in one of her schemes.

When he heard a door open, his mood lifted from reflective to impatient. She swept into his office, looking fresh, vibrant, her eyes sparkling. She didn't even bother with a good morning. After plopping on to her favourite position on the corner of his desk she demanded, 'Are you and Rosie seeing one another again?'

Surprised, he asked, 'Why?'

'Because you said you didn't have anything in common.'

'And we don't, but she was given a couple of tickets to a Melbourne Symphony Orchestra recital and asked me to go.'

'Huh,' she said. 'Don't say I haven't warned you. Mum's determined to have you as a son-in-law.'

He laughed.

'No chance of that. Even if I were interested, Rosie isn't. Now, can we get on to more important things, locating Helen Porter for example?'

She folded her arms.

'Guess what I found out? Jonesy was lying about Helen Porter. She hasn't got soft eyes. They're cold and calculating.'

'So you went sailing off to meet her after agreeing not to act without telling me first?'

'I'm sorry, but once I'd traced the house, and discovered she was at home alone, it was too good an opportunity to miss. I actually spoke to her. The woman is attractive, cool, classy, tanned, manicured from head to toe, and sharp.'

She didn't sound like the woman Jones spoke of on the tape, he thought, but there was no way he intended to encourage Kate any further. She was so gung-ho about solving the Jonesy riddle that she'd lost her perspective, any apprehension about walking into dangerous situations. Not that she had much control over her impetuous nature in the first place. That's what troubled him.

'Kate,' he said using his best courtroom voice, 'your cavalier attitude really upsets me. You've broken your promise to me. I feel as if I can't trust you any more.'

'Oh, but Dan . . . '

'But nothing. You're not going to sweet-talk me this time. If you don't go to the police, I will.'

Her face turned crimson, a suggestion of tears gathering in those normally sparkling eyes. Had he been too touchy? He softened his tone.

'You have curiosity, vitality, spirit and an adventurous nature. They make you a very special person, but one day, in your enthusiasm, it worries me that you'll go too far. We did agree twenty-four hours, didn't we?'

She scrubbed a tear from her cheek and moved to the other side of his desk to face him.

'You're my best friend, Dan, and I'm

sorry if I upset you. I'll try to curb my impulsiveness, honest.'

Touched by her sincerity, he softened his approach.

'You could start by forgetting this Jones person.'

'Please, I'm asking you to try to understand why I can't abandon my interest in him yet, and why I need your help a little longer. If someone used you the way that guy used me, you'd want to know the reason, wouldn't you?'

Her dark eyes glistened and the hardness in his heart softened. He sighed heavily.

'Fair enough, but I'd leave it to the police.'

'You know the police won't do anything until I give them something tangible to go on.'

'OK. Tell me what you have in mind.'

'The house next to the Porter's is up for sale.'

'Am I missing something?'

'I was hoping that tonight you'd . . . '

He reclined in his chair, uncomfort-able. She'd awakened his interest, had him wanting to know more about the Porter woman. He should have sent Kate packing with a warning that she'd have to move out of Writer's Cramp if she kept on about this affair.

Instead, he asked, 'Tonight, what?'

Kate leaned forward and thrust a newspaper For Sale advertisement of a mansion called Normandy House in front of him.

'I was rather hoping you and I could pose as newlyweds. You're a very successful solicitor, and . . . '

He nodded his head slowly.

'Got it. We're interested in buying the place next door to the Porters? And while we're there we try to find out more about Helen Porter?'

He shook his head when he saw the expression on her face.

'Don't even think about it, Kate. Suppose the classy Ms Porter is in the garden, or sees you through the window and recognises you?'

'You're such a worry wart.'

She patted her flat stomach.

'No baby bump, and I'm off to the hairdressers later for a new style and tint. I'm going short and blonde. Sexy, eh?'

She was incorrigible but her gameness, her full-on tilt at life tightened the knot of anxiety in his gut. She'd hustled her way into his life, become his foaming ice-cold beer after a day of unbearable heat; his blazing log fire on long, cold winter weekends, and instinctively he had become her protector. He would have to go with her, if only to ensure her safety. Still, he had to try to talk her out of it.

'If this Porter woman is around, and as sharp as you say, she could remember you. Now if I went . . . '

'Alone? No, we have to be a couple interested in buying the house. Hey, why don't you come with me to the salon and have your grey hairs touched up so you won't look too old for me?' she said with a wide grin.

He smiled.

'Very well, I'll come if only to see you don't get into any more trouble.'

'To the hairdresser's?'

'Certainly not. Would you like me to ring the estate agent, and set up an inspection of this Normandy Hall for late this afternoon? When we go, what are we looking for?'

'Love it, Dan. I think the agent could be good for a whole lot of info, especially if he sees us as potential buyers, people who've had a bad experience with neighbours before.' She giggled. 'Who knows, we might even spot Mr Porter coming or going.'

'You're interested in the husband?'

'I don't think you're that thick. If a contract is out to kill a married woman, who's the first person you'd suspect?'

'The husband.'

'As if you didn't already know, and having met his ice-maiden of a wife, it wouldn't surprise me.'

'You're talking murder, Kate. Haven't you heard of divorce?'

As she turned to leave, she delivered a self-satisfied smile.

'Aha, but divorce wouldn't deliver him bachelor status plus the business, which, I also found out yesterday, she owns. What I wouldn't give to see a copy of her will! I bet it all goes to him.'

5

As Dan drove along the busy commuter-time road to the Porter house, Kate said, 'You haven't commented on my hair.'

'Blondes with short, spiky hair and saucy noses don't appeal to me. And when your mum and dad see it they'll have apoplexy.'

'They'll live and it's only temporary. By the way, Rosie thinks I'm taking up too much of your time.'

'I agree with her one hundred per cent.'

'I thought you said you weren't seeing one another? In fact, she told me she was seeing a guy from her office.'

'You thought right on both counts. He couldn't make it to the concert last night so she asked me because she didn't want to waste the ticket.'

'So you're just good friends, as they

say in the classics? She could have asked me.'

'You weren't around. Why are you so interested anyway?'

'Just making conversation.'

It was not yet dark when they parked in front of Normandy Hall. A man in a dark suit stood on the veranda and started down the drive as they alighted from the car.

'Some property,' Dan whispered. 'It'll fetch around three million. I feel like an imposter. How did I let you talk me into this? I'm going to have to tell the agent I can't make any commitments until I talk to my bank manager.'

It pleased Kate that he seemed to be entering into the spirit of the thing.

'Play up the fact that you're a lawyer,' she suggested, linking her arm into his as they strolled up the pathway.

As the agent neared, she felt his eyes linger on her hair, saw the distaste curl his thin lips, but he extended his hand to Dan.

'Mr and Mrs Kingston, Keith Poole.

We spoke earlier on the phone. It's a little unusual, but as you asked, the owners, Colonel and Mrs Molesworth, have agreed to be here while you inspect the house.'

Kate tilted her head and offered a wide smile.

'Thank you, Mr Poole. My husband and I wanted to talk to the owners about the little personal things relating to the house. But we promise not to try to negotiate with them, don't we, darling? That wouldn't be ethical.'

'Oh, well . . . ' Dan prevaricated.

Poole pushed the doorbell and a man, once tall but now with the stoop of a well-preserved, elderly gentleman, thinning grey hair, a military moustache, opened the door. He shook Dan's hand vigorously.

'Come in, come in, Mr Kingston.'

'It's a magnificent house.'

Dan studied the papered walls, the heavy drapes and furnishings, the ceiling roses.

'Home, dear boy. It's a home.

Classical, true to its era,' the colonel enthused.

'You'll want it the minute you inspect it,' Poole added.

After a lot of enthusiastic comments as they passed from room to room, Kate looked up at Dan.

'It's beautiful, isn't it, darling? Wonderful for quiet, exclusive dinner parties with the legal fraternity.' Then turning to Colonel Molesworth, she added, 'There are a few questions I'd like to ask. I understand the people next door, the Porters, I'm told, are night owls, parties into the morning, motor-bikes revving up, that kind of thing.'

'Why, no, he's the head of a big international company, Cleveland Exports. They're very respectable people.'

Kate gave the old man a big smile.

'Gossip is so unreliable these days. Is your wife in?'

Mrs Molesworth appeared in the doorway as if she'd been eavesdropping. She eased swirls of grey hair escaping from combs back from her face.

'I do believe the wife's family is well-known in social circles and generous benefactors,' she said. 'I was taught it's rude to talk about money, but everyone around here is aware the Porters are very wealthy. Can I get you a cup of tea, Mrs Kingswood, while the men look at the games room?'

'It's Kingston, but please, call me Kate. I'd love tea, Mrs Molesworth.'

Dan glared at her, but was led off by the eager agent and the colonel to view the billiard room. Mrs Molesworth settled Kate in a comfortable chair in a small room they obviously used as a sitting-room, and eventually returned with a tray, glittering with quality china and spoons, and a plate of biscuits.

'So you have good neighbours,' Kate began, anxious to draw from Mrs Molesworth everything she was willing to give, and a bit more.

'Did I tell you the children are hers from an earlier marriage? I understand he's been married before, too. I don't hold with it, but they seem very well-suited.' The old lady sighed. 'I do hope you buy the house. It would add to the tone of the street if a judge were to move in.'

'He's not a judge, yet,' Kate chipped in, 'but he will be.'

'That's nice, dear. You must stand behind your man. I always knew Cedric would become a colonel.' She sat forward in her chair. 'I hope you won't mind me giving you a little advice, Katherine.'

Kate couldn't wait to hear.

'It's your hair, dear. Perhaps if you were to have a more traditional style? I can recommend a hairdresser down in Toorak Village. One must try to fit in.'

'Of course, but as a writer, I sometimes have to do things as an experiment.'

'A writer! How wonderful. You must never be lonely. It's very quiet here at times. Did I mention my son and his family are in England?'

'You must miss them. I expect the Porters have a lot of visitors and dinner parties.'

'Occasionally they have black-tie affairs.'

The old lady went on about the neighbours on the other side, and Kate listened politely. But when the men returned to the room, she leaped to her feet, glanced pointedly at her watch and hurried to Dan's side.

'Darling, we really mustn't keep these people any longer.'

As they moved towards the door, Mrs Molesworth caught up with Kate, and whispered, 'I don't suppose the colonel mentioned the beastly motorbike which started arriving next door in the evenings last week? His hearing's not so good these days.'

Kate drew in her breath, but managed to smile to hide her intense curiosity.

'I hope we'll see you soon, Mrs Molesworth,' she said. 'I've enjoyed talking to you.'

'Next time you call, you might bring a copy of your book?'

On their way home, Dan, wiping his

brow growled, 'How we got out of there without signing a contract beats me.'

'You're a solicitor. The only person who can talk you into anything is Rosie. But it was fun, wasn't it, imagining ourselves buying the mansion, and we learned a lot about the Porters.'

'Yeah? What?'

She laughed, and passed on the bits and pieces of information she'd received from Mrs Molesworth.

'The colonel's wife told you that? It doesn't really help, though.'

'There's more.' She couldn't keep the smugness from her voice. 'The sweet old thing is lonely cooped up in that great house and entertains herself by peeking, and listening. She heard and saw a motorbike arriving next door on several occasions last week.'

'Interesting.'

'So is this. The Porters have both been married before. The children are hers. Their father's name is Holding.'

She placed her hand on his arm.

'Can you do some research on

Cleveland Exports? They could be into importing illegal things, substances, for example. What do you think?'

'Kate, you're imagination is running away with you. You've had your fun playing detective, now you go to the police.'

'I think you're right. I'll talk to you tomorrow. Can you drop me home?'

Dan thought she'd given in too easily, which meant she had plans she wasn't sharing. Tomorrow he'd do what he should have done days ago and talk to an old detective friend, off the record.

As he parked the car, she reached up and kissed him on the cheek.

'Thanks for tonight. I know it went against your grain.'

The moonlight caught the curve of her lips. For a mad moment he thought of kissing her, but that could ruin the familiar relationship they had. He settled for grasping her gently around the arm.

'Don't barge in, will you? Warn your

parents, otherwise they're going to freak out when they see your hair.'

'Not if I tell them you think it's stunning.'

'If it'll help.'

He climbed back into the car, uncomfortable. He hoped the family wasn't assuming because he and Rosemary went out last night they were an item again. He'd make sure they understood it was a one-off, and it wouldn't happen again. As he garaged his car, he decided it would be prudent to distance himself from Katy, too, but how, when she occupied space in his rooms, in his mind?

*   *   *

Kate's office phone rang mid-morning. Even before he spoke, she recognised his smoky breathing.

'Ya haven't been to the cops like I asked ya, luv. What's holding you up?'

An anxious knot developed in her stomach. Did he have her under surveillance? If so, he'd know she'd visited the Toorak houses.

'Rubbish. You can't know what I'm doing twenty-four hours a day,' she snapped.

His laugh filled her with uncertainty.

'How ya gunna know that?'

She drew in a long breath.

'If ya don't warn the cops, the contract'll be let again and that classy dame could be history.'

His laugh sent a shiver through her.

'I'm fair dinkum, luv. You've got till five o'clock tomorrow to decide.'

His laugh echoed down the phone before it went dead. Her heart pumping, she raced to Dan's office.

'What is it?' Impatient blue eyes glinted, but his voice softened when he looked up, frowned. 'You're very pale.'

'He rang again. He's urging me to go to the police.'

'Whatever his motives, he's right, Kate. I've gone along with you to this point but it's obvious that guy's got a hidden agenda and scares you. Look, I have a detective acquaintance, Gary Marsh. I've called him and he's coming over tomorrow. I want you to talk to him off the record, show him the tape, and ask what he advises.'

She stared down at her fingernails.

'Honestly, I'm not trying to delay this, but . . . '

He leaned forward, rested one elbow on the desk, determination in his voice.

'Kate, don't test me any further on this. Step out of line once more and I promise you, you're out of Writer's Cramp. Ten o'clock tomorrow morning in my office. Yes?'

She sighed. 'If you insist.'

'I do, and until then please stay out of trouble.'

Hurrying to her little niche, Kate pushed open the door. She'd hate to lose this super little corner, so why risk getting Dan offside any more? Still, she thought positively, she had a little time left to recheck the Jonesy tape. Something about it still nagged at her. As she listened once more, she at last discovered what had troubled her about the conversation with Jonesy.

Tingling with awareness and expectation, she reached into a drawer for her file of newspaper clippings. She called it her Ideas file, for these were reports of actual happenings which had the potential to be the basis of a fiction crime story. Her fingers flicked through the cuttings. She knew exactly what she was looking for, and there it was — a human interest piece in a women's magazine about a hitman who couldn't do the deed after he came face to face with his quarry in a newsagent's.

It went on to quote him.

She smiled at me and I knew I couldn't do it. She looked nice, decent, pretty.

The story also carried a picture of the man, vaguely stooped, wearing a red check shirt, jeans, keys clipped to his pocket, scuffed elastic-sided boots and a pony tail. Kate could hardly believe it. She stared at a carbon copy of Jonesy, except this man had weathered skin and a knock-about face.

Jonesy's face was a blank, but whoever Jonesy was, he'd turned himself into that person for the meeting with her. It was yet another piece of the jigsaw, she thought, her stomach bubbling with enthusiasm. Now she knew for sure she'd been duped by a cunning man with a secret agenda. But she was yet to discover what his motive was and why he'd implicated her in his nasty little scheme.

Dan called Kate into his office an hour before Marsh was due, to discuss their tactics.

'Kate, we're going to hand the problem over to him so you can get on with your novel, and I can get on with my practice. You've been chasing shadows for days now and it hasn't got you anywhere.'

'But it's been absorbing, chasing those shadows. And I have gathered quite a few ideas for future novels. I'm only sorry that I haven't yet got to the bottom of things.'

He smiled and tapped her affectionately on her nose.

'I understand where you're coming from, but one day your passion for a good story will get you into serious trouble.'

Kate loved the way he touched her, the warmth of his eyes upon her. She didn't quite know how or when it had happened, but the recognition that he'd become so important to her, indeed integral to her very existence, shook her. Her mouth dried up.

'Really, I'll be fine,' she mumbled.

He shook his head.

'One day you mightn't. Now, today we let Marsh ask the questions. Answer them as you remember things, and volunteer the tape. He's promised our chat will be off the record. OK?'

He leaned back in his chair, signalling the discussion was over and this time she decided not to argue.

'So where do we start? There's so much to tell.'

'Tell it as it happened. You thought

Jonesy was a prankster. You didn't believe him, but you decided to meet him. Marsh will ask why. Tell me in your own words how you'll answer.'

'I'm a tad impulsive. I never shy away from a challenge, and besides, he suggested I'd get the material for a good story, and my creative juices had dried up. I honestly didn't really think he'd show, but just in case, I attached the tape recorder to my car's floor. Even when he arrived, I thought he was having me on, taking the joke a bit further.'

'Good, take your time over your answers and don't let Marsh fluster or unsettle you.'

Dan placed his hand over hers. She felt warm and contented and safe.

'Kate Drewett get flustered?' she queried, smiling across at him.

'Not likely, eh?' He tilted her chin with a finger. 'Pretend you're your lady detective. She'd answer confidently.'

He brushed his hand over her spiky hair. How she wished his feelings were more than those of a big brother, now that Rosie was no longer interested. She dragged herself from the desk.

'Sometimes I think you understand me better than I understand myself.'

She detected the faint sound of a sigh before he said, 'So do I, but even though you're far too adventurous for your own good, at heart you're a sweet kid.'

If only he didn't think of her as a skittish young woman, who lacked all the social graces and a sense of responsibility. It filled her with a longing, on the edge of melancholy and regret, that she had not been given some of her sister's poise and personality.

Unsettled by her thoughts, she strolled across to the window, anxious for Marsh to arrive, and gazing down on a busy street, her mind sprung back to reality and her spirits rose as she called to mind she as yet hadn't told Dan what she'd discovered about Jonesy from her cuttings.

Hearing her name called, she swung

around to see a man, tall, portly, a second chin sagging over his shirt collar, scant, wind-blown grey hair framing a large, florid face. But it was his light blue eyes, lie-detector eyes, she thought, which unsettled her. You've got nothing to fear, you're not going to lie, she reminded herself.

'Off the record?' Dan said insistently as he indicated Gary Marsh to sit down. 'You agreed earlier.'

The detective sank into a chair, filled its space, as if he'd been sculpted into it.

'Sure thing. Later, the little lady can come down to the station if necessary and make a formal statement. I'll take a few notes of our little chat if it's OK with you. But first, Dan, you gave me the registration number of a motorbike.'

Kate's body tensed as she waited for him to go on. How on earth had she forgotten Dan had promised to follow up on the bike Jonesy rode?

'It's registered to a Drew Rawlings. He's a broken-down footballer, works as a courier. No police record.'

'He could be Jonesy and you're not even going to interview him?' she demanded to know with a rush.

'Let me ask the questions, little lady.'

Kate's thoughts took wing. Who was Drew Rawlings and what was his connection with Helen Porter? Where did she come into the conundrum?

'Are you listening, Kate?' Dan cut in. 'Detective Inspector Marsh asked you when you received the first phone call.'

'Sorry.'

She felt easier by the minute as the expected questions flowed, for all he did was grunt after each response, make notes, and move on.

Finally, snapping his notebook shut, he said, 'That's about it for now.'

Kate didn't realise she'd been holding her breath between answers until that moment. She breathed out, felt the rush of air tickle her nose.

'Really?'

'One other thing,' he said as he stood up.

'Yes?'

'If you thought this mystery man was fair dinkum, why didn't you come to the police?'

His lie-detector eyes caught hers. She blushed.

'I wasn't one hundred per cent sure, so I kind of decided . . . Dan urged me to report it, but I'm a crime novelist. I mean . . . ' She stumbled again over the reply. 'I apologise. I should have.'

'You say this guy asked you to go to the police. Are you sure of that?'

'It's on the tape.'

Dan spoke for the first time.

'Let Gary hear the tape, Kate.'

Kate motioned to the recorder which she'd set up on a filing cabinet. Marsh placed it on the desk and activated it. They huddled around it.

'It's pretty scratchy, but you can clearly hear what he says,' Kate felt the need to say.

Marsh was smiling once it finished.

'It's a hoax. The guy's a con. We get these knock-about nut cases regularly.

They're out of work and looking for some kicks.'

'It's not that simple. Didn't you notice he forgets to speak in that rough manner every now and again?' Kate protested.

Marsh's lie-detector eyes narrowed.

'Play it again and listen for flaws in his street-wise speech. Every now and then 'ya' becomes 'you' and so on.'

'Very well.'

Marsh sat back down, activated the tape again, and they sat in studied silence as it replayed. At the end, Marsh raised his brows.

'You're right, little lady, but whoever said an educated man couldn't orchestrate a hoax on a struggling writer?'

Kate didn't take too kindly to him referring to her as a little lady and a struggling writer. She tossed her head and glared at Dan.

'I know you're amused, but there are a few more things I've found out about Jonesy,' she said.

'OK, little lady, convince me this

educated guy has a secret agenda.'

Kate wanted to tell him she wasn't his little lady but why bother? He was about to find out she couldn't be tossed off as an impressionable, young writer. She began slowly, anxious to include everything.

'I keep newspaper clipping of real-life dramas, most writers do, in an Ideas file. They're a source of possible story lines. Ever since I met Jonesy, I've had this odd feeling he wasn't real, and yesterday, it finally came to me. In my file, I found a cutting I'd clipped from a women's magazine, detailing the human interest story of a hitman who ran into his proposed victim in a shop by accident, and liked her. The article ran a picture of the man. He was dressed almost identically to Jonesy on the day I met him, except for the helmet. I'm convinced he'd read that article and was playing a rôle, but why?'

'Interesting,' Dan whispered.

'Do you really have to ask why?' Marsh said gruffly. 'Because the man's a harmless nut case who reads women's magazines. It's a pattern.'

Desperately disappointed that her revelations were dismissed one by one as dross, Kate stood up, and confronted him, her eyes fiery.

'I'm sorry you think I'm wasting your time,' she said, and seizing the tape from the recorder, she thrust it into Marsh's hand. 'You're going to need this later when you find how wrong you've been.'

Turning on her heels, she marched out, leaving Dan and Marsh shrugging and more than a little uncertain.

6

To Dan's surprise, on the way down in the lift, Marsh said, 'I'm thinking of paying an informal call on Mr Rawlings. Can't do any harm to check him out, and it might just keep the little lady happy. I wouldn't really have thought Ms Drewett was your type, mate, but she's a smart little filly, perky, too.'

Dan brushed him off.

'You're right on both counts. She's smart, and she's not my type. What gave you the idea she was?'

'In my job, you get to read the signs, the body language, and in your case those signs stick out like a sore toe.' He laughed with gusto, before offering his hand to Dan and saying, 'I'll get back if there's anything to report.'

'I'm relying on you to take a serious look into this business. Kate is impulsive, but she has an intuitive mind, and you have to admit there are some very odd things about this affair.'

A man of few words, Marsh replied, 'I'll make a few enquiries.'

While returning to his office, Dan tried to dismiss Marsh's suggestion that he'd fallen for Kate, but the idea circled on in his head. Inside the office he found Kate lounging back in his chair. She'd bounced back from her little attack of frustration, as she always did.

Wiping her brow with a theatrical flourish, she said, 'I'm relieved that's over, the inspector is quite fearsome. I bet he gave you an earful about me, including that I've got a vivid imagination.'

'Actually, I think he likes you.'

'Bosh.'

'I've got a bone to pick with you.'

'Be my guest,' she said, interest lighting her eyes.

'You kept all that stuff about Jonesy to yourself, left me out on a limb.'

'Not intentionally. I only worked it

out late yesterday and we got caught up with other things this morning.'

'Is there anything else you haven't told me?'

'May I remind you, you didn't mention you had Marsh checking the motorbike registration. This Drew Rawlings who owned it could be Jonesy. Dan,' she said, a finger at the side of her mouth as if deep in thought, 'why don't you take me out to dinner tonight so we can discuss it?'

'Should I suspect an ulterior motive?'

'The last thing Mum said as I raced out this morning was, 'Ask Dan back for dinner, and don't monopolise his time when he gets here.' That can only mean there's a roast on and she hasn't given up trying to get you and Rosie back together. Frankly I'm a little tired of my mother's matchmaking schemes.'

Kate had an infuriating smile on her lips, a smile which suggested she knew exactly what she was doing. She was different from her sister. She had an openness, a lively imagination and an ability to make him laugh. He gazed at her now. She'd taken over his chair again and swung back and forth like a child, and yet the lively, headstrong kid was no more.

Now he saw a lovely young woman, a young woman who stirred and confused his emotions. She'd worked her way, almost surreptitiously, into his heart, and unsettled him, but of one thing he felt very certain, if he were ever to experience the comfort and peace of belonging, she would have to play a major rôle.

'I'll talk to your mother when I pick you up for dinner. I'll assure her, as tactfully as possible, that Rosemary and I have agreed we don't have a future together,' he said.

'You don't mind being seen dining with a punk rocker?' She grinned as she patted her spiky blonde hair. 'I've got a great idea. Why don't we stop off at the Dinkum Inn for a drink first? I haven't been there in an age. It's such a friendly old pub and I can introduce you to lots of writers and musicians who gather there.'

'Sure, if that's what you'd like.'

Writers and musicians weren't his meat, yet he felt absurdly lighthearted, energised at the thought of taking her out.

He escorted her to the carpark and opened her car door. Her dark eyes gleamed as she thanked him. He was kidding himself if he thought this was merely a dinner date. She had something else in mind at the Dinkum Inn, but in his present mood, so what?

'I'll pick you up at seven,' he said.

That evening, as they made their way into the inn, Dan said, 'I'm relieved Rosemary's convinced your mother she's found herself a gorgeous man, and there was never anything serious between us. Your mother didn't seem too disappointed.'

'Especially when she knew you and I were going out to dinner tonight. One way or another she's determined to have you as a son-in-law.'

He smiled. 'Your mother has always had good taste in men.'

'You like Dad, too?'

'He's a good bloke.'

A group of people interrupted them and called to Kate. She moved forward, her eyes shining. Dan restrained her gently by placing his hand on her arm.

'I'd like to spend at least part of the evening alone talking with you.'

'You would?'

'I thought we should celebrate the end of the Jonesy affair.'

'It won't be the end for me until I understand what it was all about.'

'Now, Kate . . .'

Someone called her name again, waved her across.

'Can we just say hello? You'll like them, they're a friendly bunch.'

'Lead on. I have an uneasy feeling this could turn into a long night.'

She laughed. 'Not necessarily.' Then taking his hand, she led him to a crowded table and introduced him to a sea of faces as the man who had given her Writer's Cramp! They enjoyed the joke before the tall thin one with the long, wispy hair clamoured, 'Grab a coupla chairs, mate. What'll you have?'

'Thanks, but we're not staying,' Kate said, promptly sitting down. Then she turned her wide-eyed glance up to Dan. 'We could have one drink. It's so long since I've spent time with the crowd. Squeeze in here next to me.'

She patted half her chair. Dan resigned himself. After all, being ambushed by Kate's literary friends didn't really surprise him. This was a popular watering hole where writers and artists gathered. He eased on to the edge of the chair, felt her warmth next to him.

'Get the bloke a seat before he falls through the cracks,' someone said, and everybody shuffled along as another chair appeared at the other side of the table. 'Make yourself comfy, mate. You're gonna be here a while once Katy settles in,' someone said.

Dan tried to laugh, but he felt anything but amused. If he had to be here, he wanted to stay close to Kate. But he decided to go quietly, until she piped up.

'It's musical chairs time, gang. Everybody move one seat to the left,' and in the riot of shuffling chair legs and bodies, she said softly to Dan, 'I prefer being next to you.'

'Me, too,' he whispered into her hair.

He replaced his arm around her, claiming her as his partner. She smiled her approval as a round of foaming beers arrived, which he insisted on paying. They started talking about football, but soon settled into serious discussions, starting with the latest literary awards. Dan began to appreciate their knowledge and range of opinions, and to enjoy the lively exchange of words.

Occasionally he contributed to the debates. Kate was sounding off about the latest political situation when he glanced up at her. He didn't quite know why, but he only had to look at her these days to feel a bit weak at the knees. Later tonight, they'd be alone. Should he tell her how important she'd become to him, and hope it didn't interfere with the close relationship they already had?

Kate had turned to one of her friends, Shelley.

'How's the writing, Shell? Had any poems published lately?'

'I'm thinking of self-publishing. Getting quotes, potential orders from friends. What's your Fabian Farley investigating at the moment?'

Dan heard Kate draw in her breath, her voice eager.

'A football crime. Your dad was a coach, wasn't he? He might be able to help with my research. In my clippings file, I found a story about a Drew Rawlings, a broken-down footballer who retired early because of injury. I'm using him as inspiration for my story of such a character who turns bitter, aimless and winds up dead.'

'Great idea, Kate. As a matter of fact, I remember Drew Rawlings quite well.

A good looker, but he turned out to be a born loser — lost his wife, his home, the lot after he gave up the game,' Shelley said.

As simply as that, Jonesy was back on the agenda. Irritation stirred Dan's stomach. They were supposed to be celebrating the end of the Jonesy affair, yet obviously Kate's reason for suggesting they come to the Dinkum Inn was to sound out her friends, many of them football fans, about this Rawlings character who owned the motorcycle.

'I met him a few times,' Shelley was saying. 'My dad felt sorry for him. Poor bloke could have been quite wealthy. While he lasted, he made real money in the game and through promotions,' Shelley said.

'So why did he retire?'

Dan touched Kate's arm.

'I thought we came out to enjoy the evening.'

'Just a couple more questions. This is interesting stuff. Did you say why he stopped playing football, Shell?'

By now, the attention of the entire group focused on Shelley.

'I'm not sure but he was injury prone. He was in and out of the team for months, and finally dropped from the squad. He was devastated, still young. He thought the club owed him something.'

Dan sighed, but Kate's eyes gleamed.

'What did he do after he retired?'

'Dad could tell you.'

Dan placed his hand under Kate's elbow, applied a little pressure.

'We should be going.'

Thankfully, she stood up without any further persuasion.

'Thanks, Shell, I've give your dad a call. Gotta go, guys. Catch you later.'

Then, as an afterthought, she turned again to Shelley.

'By the way, I meant to ask. Do you happen to know if Rawlings smokes?'

'Not while he was playing football. The coach wouldn't have tolerated it.'

Dan noticed Kate's eyes glint and as they walked to the door he said,

'Chasing shadows again, Kate?'

'You're cross with me?'

'Yes. You chose the Dinkum Inn because you came here tonight to do some more probing. You knew your friend's father was a football coach, and dimwitted me, I thought we came out together to celebrate the end of the Jonesy affair. I should have known.'

'Dan, we did come to celebrate, but maybe different things.'

'What are you celebrating, Kate?'

'I've wanted you to ask me out for ages.'

'Why didn't you say so?'

'Too shy, I guess. You wouldn't have taken me seriously.'

He laughed, happy, his displeasure disappearing like a whiff of smoke.

'You haven't got a shy bone in your body.'

'But this is different. I'm not good at relationships,' then, as if to change the subject, she added, 'I'm only good at curiosity, and stuff like that.'

Could she feel more for him than

sisterly love? He decided not to push it, but placed his arm around her. She circled hers about him, and they strolled along the pavement.

'Curiosity is something you have down to a fine art,' he said, 'and you know what? I can't imagine you any other way. Still, I thought your question about Rawlings smoking was a waste of time. He could have taken it up after his career finished.'

She looked up at him.

'Or Jonesy may never have smoked,' she said.

He decided not to question her enigmatic statement.

'Where to from here?' he asked. 'I don't eat out much these days.'

'Me neither. We have so much in common, don't we?'

'Let's try Fleur's. Taxi,' he called with a flourish of his free arm, deciding they were wasting time.

Inside the cab, in the darkness, he cupped her adorable face gently in his hands and tilted it so that he looked into the depths of her eyes.

'Kate, I don't know how it happened, but I'm falling in love with you. Do you mind?'

She looked up at him, her eyes lighting up.

'It happened because we're having so much fun. Admit it.'

'You exasperate me sometimes. Can we be serious for a change?'

'I am. It's good having you around, but you're far too old and conservative to keep up with me long distance,' she said in a teasing tone.

He hid a secret smile, quietly encouraged by the light in her eyes, the way she snuggled up to him. She'd confessed to being shy when it came to men and he was starting to believe her. From experience, he knew that when uncomfortable, she often resorted to facetious responses.

The taxi driver broke into his thoughts.

'Hey, mate, how many times do I have to tell you we're here? The metre's ticking over.'

'Who cares?' Dan said with confidence.

After paying off the driver, he placed his arm around her. She nuzzled into him as they strolled into the restaurant. A wave of happiness cascaded over him.

Next morning, Kate felt different, excited, keen to get to the office to see Dan. Was this what being in love meant, or was it simply that she was flattered to think he could fall in love with someone as unsophisticated as her?

She avoided her parents. They would see the happiness in her eyes, the bloom in her cheeks and ask why. As she dashed out, she shouted from the front door.

'I'll get breakfast on the run,' she called to ease her mother's mind, as Mrs Drewett insisted a hearty breakfast set you up for the day.

Kate had only one problem. Once her and Dan's relationship developed, she'd have to sacrifice her cosy little Writer's Cramp. Being so close to him every day wouldn't work for her, but it was one reason, indeed the only reason, she'd be prepared to give it up. She tried to concentrate on other things as she drove across the city, and as usual found her thoughts back on Jonesy.

As the conversation she'd had with Shelley drifted through her mind, she swung the car back towards the city and the public library. There was something she needed to research. Dan would accuse her of chasing more shadows, but she could not come to any harm doing this, and it might satisfy her burning need to know.

In the section dedicated to newspaper files, she consulted one of the assistants and was soon scrolling through microfiles of the sports pages. In a sports-mad city like Melbourne, she easily located story after story of Drew Rawlings' courageous exploits on the football field, and the fall-out from his untimely retirement. His aggressive approach to the game had brought him success and for a short while he'd become a household name. But, she discovered, early arthritis had badly damaged his joints, in particular his hands. Kate asked for photocopies of a couple of the reports, and drove back to Writer's Cramp, troubled and uncertain.

Why wouldn't the police take the Jonesy affair seriously? The investigating she'd done had already uncovered so many contradictions, and until the truth could be found, she felt a heaviness in her heart that the affair would continue to haunt her, continue to disrupt her life and her ability to concentrate on her novel. Was Helen Porter's life really in danger, and why was she implicated?

She'd more or less promised Dan she'd forget the whole unpleasant experience, and if she lost Dan . . .

What should she do? If only she had someone she could sit down with and talk through her dilemma. Back in the anonymity of her office, on impulse, following a line of enquiry she'd had in mind all morning, she picked up the phone and called Cleveland Exports, purporting to be an old school friend on a visit to Melbourne, anxious to catch up for lunch tomorrow with Helen and Brian. Mr Porter, she was told, was working from home for the next few days as his wife had to fly to Asia on business. Kate left a fictitious name and hung up.

Knowing Brian Porter was at home had possibilities; she tried to deny them, to push them aside, for Dan's sake, and yet after several hours they persisted.

First stop home, where she bundled together a few bits and pieces and hurried away before her mother could delay her with searching questions about last night and her dinner with Dan. Returning to the office, she went inside trying to control the nervous anticipation bubbling inside her. She tried to pretend this was just another day. Stopping by Jill's desk, she asked, in a whisper, if she could borrow her car.

'Now what are you up to?' Jill questioned.

Touching her nose to indicate she was sharing a secret, she replied, 'Just taking a quick trip out to ... er ... better if you don't know. I'll be back before Dan even realises I'm not here. So, can I use your car?'

'You're going back to the Porter place, aren't you? Kate, is that wise?'

She laughed, joked, an attack of nerves drawing the skittish responses.

'You think your car might break down?'

'That's not what I mean and you know it.'

Kate titled her chin with determination.

'When have you known me to be wise?'

Jill shrugged, but handed her the keys and checked her watch.

'OK, on condition if you're not back within the hour, I inform Dan.'

'Be a pal and give me ninety minutes before you send out the cavalry.'

'You know I could lose my job over this. Not a minute more, and be careful.'

Hurrying out the front entrance, her mind on the events ahead, she bumped straight into Dan on his way in. She'd been caught out. Her face burned, but he seemed not to notice. He smiled warmly at her.

'You're um . . . um . . . late,' she garbled.

'I'm sorry. I had to see a client first thing this morning. I'm glad you missed me. Do you still love me?'

He kept his voice low, for her only. Her heart raced. She was about to mislead Dan again. She called on the courage to speak.

'For ever, Dan,' she said softly.

'Can we talk in my office in half an hour, about our future plans?'

Oh, no! She probably wasn't going to be back in half an hour.

'I have to go out for a little while,' she managed, before glancing at her watch, 'but I must leave now or I'll be late.'

He touched her hand, concern in his dark blue eyes.

'Sweetheart, are you all right? You

look upset. Has anything happened to change things?'

'Everything's fine, but we can't talk on the doorstep. I'll pop into your office the minute I get back.'

Turning, she made a dash for her car.

7

Decidedly uneasy, Dan looked into Kate's room for the umpteenth time, but she still hadn't returned. Where was she? He had a sickening feeling that the conversation they'd exchanged earlier had something to do with the Jonesy affair. Surely she hadn't gone off on yet another reckless errand.

Striding down the passage to reception, he approached Jill.

'Any idea where Kate went? She still hasn't returned.'

Jill's face flared.

'She didn't say, but she hasn't been gone long.'

'I'm aware of that. Come on, Jill, she talks to you and it's obvious you have some idea what she's up to.'

'Honestly, she didn't actually say, but I got the impression she was planning another visit to the Porter house. She

123

borrowed my car.'

'What on earth . . . you should have told me the minute I walked in.'

'She's my friend. I tried to talk her out of it, but it's like talking to a cat with the scent of a mouse in his nostrils.'

'Tell me about it! If I were you, I'd question the friendship of that young lady. She had no right to place you in this position.'

'I did tell her I'd speak to you if she didn't get back within ninety minutes.'

Dan glanced at his watch.

'But she's only been gone ten minutes. I may be able to waylay her.'

'I hope you can.'

'Call me on the mobile if she arrives back here. She didn't happen to say why she was going?'

'I didn't ask because I didn't want to know.'

Anxious, frustrated, Dan strode back to his office to retrieve his coat, his mind crowded with disturbing scenarios. If anything happened to her . . .

What the devil was she doing out at Toorak anyway? It was a silly question to ask himself for he already had the answer. She'd become fixated on trying to unmask Jonesy, no matter the consequences.

★ ★ ★

Kate felt shaky. Her heart ached because she was deceiving Dan yet she drove herself on, and a distance from the office, pulled into a parking bay beside parkland. There she changed into hiking shoes, an old overcoat, and a long brown wig, borrowed from Rosemary's wardrobe. She dragged it back from her face and tied it with a ribbon.

Adding a pair of her mother's glasses, a quick glance in the car mirror told her she'd achieved the effect she sought. But when she looked more closely, an image of troubled eyes, of a foolish young woman, reflected back at her, even through the glasses. She loved

Dan, yet she was contemplating a reckless scheme against his wishes. How could their relationship survive such foolhardy, single-minded behaviour?

Trust between a couple was needed if a relationship were to have any chance. Dan had once suggested he found it hard to trust her, and here she was about to give him every reason to doubt her honesty again. Yanking off the glasses, she restarted the engine, and swinging across the road drove, back to the office.

Dan was about to leave his office to go in search of Kate when the sound of footsteps in the passageway cut through his confusion. He recognised them as Kate's and his heart leaped. Thank goodness she was safe.

Stay calm, he promised himself. Don't come down on her straight away. Give her a chance to explain. He hurried into the corridor, seized her by the arm and urged her into his office, and once inside, he picked up the phone, informed

Jill they weren't to be interrupted, and closed the door. Despite telling himself not to hassle her straight away, he could no longer hold back.

'What the devil are you doing in that ridiculous wig and charity shop get-up and where the devil have you been?'

He stared harshly at her and for the first time noticed how pale she looked. He strode to her side, alarmed, and without waiting for an answer, said in a concerned voice, 'Kate, you look awful.'

He noticed her shiver.

'It's these funny old clothes I'm wearing. They don't do anything for me,' she tried to joke.

'I have to agree, so tell me what you're doing in them. Come on, sweetheart, you can open up to me. What's going on?'

Her usual energy was missing from her voice.

'To be honest, I'm starting to realise what a fool I've been.' She shrugged. 'But it's nothing a really big hug won't fix.'

'One big hug coming up.'

He placed his arms about her. The wig shifted noticeably and she dragged it off her head as he held her close while they crossed to his chair. There he sat her down.

'I'm not even going to ask where you got the wig,' he said, trying to inject some levity into the tense atmosphere.

'It's Rosie's.'

'She's into wigs? I never noticed.'

'There are a lot of things you don't notice. You hadn't noticed until last night that I'm a woman. You work too hard.'

'Kate, we have to talk. I don't want to push you, but let me get you a hot drink, then we talk.' On his way out to the tearoom, he said, to lighten things, 'I had noticed you are a woman, but you kept telling me I was too old for you.'

She had the suggestion of a smile on her lips as she nodded and tucked herself farther into his chair.

Dan returned with two mugs of

steaming tea, smiled reassuringly as he placed one into slightly unsteady hands and held it there until he felt confident she'd grasped it. He took her usual seat on the corner of the desk, his legs resting on the floor and observed her quietly, distressed to find her so languid, out-of-character and compliant.

She took a few sips of the drink, and, controlling his impatience, he suggested, 'Take your time.'

'Dan, I have to know who Jonesy is. I think you're starting to understand that. The man used me, and I simply have to know why.'

'But, sweetheart, you have to let go. Leave it to Marsh to find out. I can see that whatever you were up to today is starting to effect you deeply.'

'Because it suddenly hit home that not telling you what I was doing could ruin things for us, and I couldn't bear that. You mean too much to me. Dan, I'm sorry I went off without saying, but true to form, I acted first and thought later.' She turned her face up to him, appealed, with dark misty eyes. 'Forgive me?'

He leaned forward, held her hands.

'How can I not when you look at me with those appealing eyes? Now take a few deep breaths and tell me what happened earlier. Afterwards, we can decide how we'll deal with it.'

The corners of her mouth tilted slightly. She slipped back into the chair, and folded her arms across her chest as if cold.

'If you're sure you're not mad at me.'

He flourished his hands, smiled gently.

'Scout's honour, I'm not mad at you.'

Another hesitant smile and she started.

'This morning, I spent time in the city library researching newspaper clippings about Drew Rawlings.'

'What were you looking for?'

'Anything that might point to him being Jonesy.'

'And you drew a blank, so you

decided to go off to the Porter house again,' he asked, his voice tending to sound disappointed.

'I didn't draw a blank. I found out quite a lot of interesting stuff about Rawlings. That's why I was so anxious to return to the Porter house. But I got part of the way there and thought about us and how I'd be deceiving you and you'd have every right to tell me you couldn't marry someone you can't trust. So I turned around and came back to the office,' she said spreading her arms. 'I won't pretend I'm not disappointed that I can't do this one last piece of investigating, but if the price of giving it up is having your love and trust, I'll take you every time.'

He put out his arms to her, and in silence they clung to one another. He wondered why it had taken him so long to discover her. After a short while, he stroked her hair back from her face.

'Could we chase this last shadow together and see if we can't finally put the Jones' saga to rest?'

The sparkle back in her eyes, she whispered. 'When I was driving out to Toorak, I found myself wishing I had an understanding friend with whom I could talk over these things. It's only just dawned on me that you're my friend, the person I've always been able to talk to. I've been so blind.'

He smiled down at her.

'I've had a few blind spots myself. So do you like my idea of being your sidekick for this one last tilt at discovering the truth?'

'I love it, but if you're suggesting that you come with me up to the house . . . '

Her confidence had returned, she was back on top of things.

'Only to ensure you don't get into any trouble.'

'OK, but you'd need to stay in the car.'

'I hope you're not planning to do anything illegal.'

'You know I'd never be that crazy.'

Over dinner that evening, Kate

outlined her plan.

'We borrow Jill's car because both ours have already been out there and could be recognised. You stay in the car and use binoculars to keep watch on things,' she told him.

'And what will you be doing, pray?'

'Talking to Helen Porter's husband.'

'No dice. We go up to the house together or not at all.'

'But it's my plan.'

'No, sweetheart, it's our plan. We do this together or not at all.'

'Oh, very well. You can come up to the house but I insist you don't do any talking. I have everything worked out in my mind and if you start chipping in it might mess up the plan. And by the way, you can't wear a business suit. You'll need an old pair of jeans, a worn windproof jacket and scuffed boots or trainers.'

'You'll have to head me in the direction of the nearest charity shop,' he said, grinning.

'You're enjoying this, aren't you?'

'I'll enjoy it more when our friend, Jonesy, is outed and we can get on with our lives together. Now, when we get to the house, what are we looking for?'

'Nothing. Leave everything to me.'

8

Next morning, as they drove out to Toorak, in Jill's car, Kate couldn't hide her excitement. She spoke quickly.

'I like the look — the scruffy hair and clothes, it's a change from the old dark suit and tie,' she said, nervously flicking the strap on the sleeve of his jacket. 'Is it safe to be driving while you're wearing those glasses?'

'They're my driving glasses, Kate.'

'Now, you remember everything I told you to do?' she pressed him.

'There's nothing to remember. I'm just to stand there like a tailor's dummy, listen and not utter a word. It's going to be tough, but I did all right when we went to the Molesworth house, didn't I?'

'Just checking. This visit is more important than anything else I've done in my effort to uncover who Jonesy is and what he's on about.'

'Slow down, Kate, you're too hyped up,' he said, as he halted the car outside the Porter house. 'Take a few deep breaths. We can't have you fluffing your lines.'

It was excellent advice and she took it before leaving the vehicle, but still her heart beat as loudly as a heavy metal band, her hands sweaty as she clutched the newspaper.

The street was deserted. Even a breeze gusting through the trees along the street, teasing her wig, couldn't mask the eerie silence. How glad she was that she had Dan by her side. She chanced a glance at the Molesworth house, which still displayed the **For Sale** sign outside. Could the lonely old lady be watching from a window? If she were, she would see only a nondescript man and woman trudging up the driveway of the Porter home.

It was the thought of meeting Brian Porter that gave the knot of anxiety in her stomach. How often had she wondered what he was like? Would he answer the door? Could she hold him in conversation long enough to fulfil her mission? Faking weary steps, as planned, they plodded up the pebbled drive. She whispered to Dan.

'Do you get the feeling that a thousand eyes are watching us and we're never going to reach the front door?'

'You're OK, Kate, I won't let anything happen to you.'

At last they stepped on to the veranda. She glanced at Dan, who stood slightly behind her and with shaky fingers she pressed the button. When she heard footsteps inside, she straightened her shoulders in an effort to calm her nerves and prepare herself.

The man who opened the door was tallish, middle-aged, his dark hair greying at the sides and forehead. Her mother would have described him as a distinguished-looking gentleman, but only until she saw the superior eyebrows, his icy stare. The man had no warmth. His lips curled with an ugly astuteness when he spoke.

'Yes?' His question sounded more like a demand.

'Mr Porter?'

He narrowed his eyes.

'Yes.'

'I usually see Mrs Porter. She always buys one. I'm representing the . . . '

'Call back another time and talk to her. I haven't got time to waste.'

He began to close the door. She dropped the church newsletter as she prepared to force it on to him. It fell across the doorstep. Dan leaped to pick it up and she stepped across and got in his way.

'Oh, dear, how careless of me. I'm sorry,' she muttered as Porter retrieved it and thrust it back to her.

'Take your paper and get off my premises. I've got no time for this kind of thing. Religion should be sold in churches, not door-to-door,' he barked.

What a strange way to think of it, Kate thought. Normally, she'd have challenged his statement, but today she had more important things on her mind. Excitement stirring in her stomach, she managed to reply.

'Thank you, we'll call again,' and smiling at Dan, they turned to leave.

Though her emotional state urged her to dash to the car, she hissed to Dan, 'Take it slowly. He may be watching from indoors and we mustn't look intimidated or appear anxious to get away.'

Only when they climbed into the vehicle could she breathe easily.

'Well,' Dan said, 'that was a total waste of time. Darned if I know what you were trying to achieve.'

'You almost mucked it up,' she said brightly.

He started the car and eased it out on to the road.

'Excuse me? How could I when I didn't say a word?'

'You were spot on about not saying anything. Anyway, no need to worry, everything turned out all right.'

'Come on, Kate,' he complained, 'stop teasing. What the devil was that little pantomime all about? I thought we were partners.'

'It's complicated and the traffic's heavy at the moment. You should be concentrating on the road. Let's wait until we get back at the office.'

'You're enjoying this, aren't you?' he said, pulling into a vacant car space.

She laughed quietly.

'You could say that. So why have we stopped here?'

'Because I want answers. We're going to find somewhere to have coffee.'

'We can't go into a shop wearing this gear. We look ridiculous.'

'Porter had to put up with us.'

Kate removed the glasses and wig and fluffed up her hair before she stepped from the car. Amused by their appearance, they strolled along the shopping strip arm in arm until they found a small café and went in. Dan ordered two coffees and they engaged in small talk until they arrived.

'OK, you have five minutes to give me this so-called complicated explanation of today's pointless exercise.'

Kate grinned, covered her hand over his.

'It wasn't useless. As a matter of fact, I know for certain now who Jonesy is.'

Dan leaned back in his chair and his hand slipped from her hold.

'OK, I'm sufficiently interested to ask who he is.'

She leaned forward, spoke in an eager whisper.

'Porter.'

He raised his brows.

'Yeah. Now convince me.'

'This morning, I went to the state library and researched the newspaper files and discovered why Drew Rawlings retired from football. He had severe arthritis in his hands which limited his capacity to mark the ball. That ruled him out as Jonesy.'

Dan frowned. 'It did?'

'Yes, because I remembered something about our mystery man which I hadn't thought of before. You see, when I met him that day at Northland, he was heavily disguised, but I did see one part of him. Its importance only struck me the other day after we'd discussed the things we knew about Jonesy. Do you remember I said the only parts of his body I saw were his hands?'

'Vaguely.'

'When he removed his riding gloves, he slapped them against his hands. I can still conjure up the picture, the sound. They were not arthritic hands, nor were they hands of a manual worker or a smoker.'

He sat forward, and spoke in a subdued tone.

'Kate, are you sure?'

'Absolutely. They were long, lean hands, and here's something else which can't be disputed. I'm kicking myself now because I didn't see the significance of it. On the side of his right thumb he had a small scar, as if he'd had surgery to remove a skin cancer.'

She paused for breath before going

on, hardly able to stem the flow of words.

'This was no down-and-out hitman. How could I have missed the clues? His street-wise speech, the odour of smoke, the pony tail and clothes were so obviously fake, as was the yarn he pitched about Helen Porter being nice. She's anything but. When I was sitting next to Porter in my car, I had the strangest feeling that it wasn't happening, that he was a ghostly figure, but I had put it down to the eerie encounter. Now I know there was no such person as this Jones.'

She grinned with satisfaction.

'Clever old me, eh? Now all we have to do is find out what Porter's up to, and why he involved me.'

'Well done. So we rule out Rawlings as our man.'

'Absolutely. Porter is Jonesy. If necessary, I'll swear on a stack of bibles the hands I saw earlier today when he picked up the newspaper were the same as Jonesy's.'

Dan took a long drink of his coffee.

'So that was your little plan, and that's why I nearly messed it up by trying to get to the paper first? You, Kate Drewett, have a very persistent and inventive mind. No wonder I'm going grey. Thank goodness you didn't go off on your own.'

'Our next step is to find out how Rawlings and Porter are connected.'

'Why?'

'Because the motorbike was registered in Rawlings' name, yet Porter rode it.'

'We don't have to do anything of the sort. I'm going to call Marsh, and you're going to give him this latest piece of information and he's going to take it from here.'

'Dan,' she wailed, 'please don't stop me now. I'm on the verge of something big.'

'Marsh has the facilities. He can check Porter's health records and verify the scar on his thumb for a start.'

'But will he? Haven't I proved I know what I'm doing?'

'No, you've proved you take far too many risks for my liking.'

He smiled and wrapped her hand in his.

'Let's get back to the office. I want to hold you and kiss you.'

She looked up at him, smiled through tear-glazed eyes.

'I didn't realise quite how much grief I give you.'

But it didn't stop her from still protesting as they strolled from the coffee shop into the street.

'Dan, I'm on top of this. We only need another few hours and betcha we can discover that Jonesy, I mean Porter, is planning to kill his superior wife and inherit her money. Why would we want to go back to work now?'

'You're out of luck. You can't get around me any more, Ms Drewett. I refuse to be conned by those innocent eyes and pouty lips ever again. You choose me or Jonesy.'

'Oh, Dan. It's you, of course, it's you, but . . . '

He put his finger to her lips, shook his head.

'No buts. Now, let's go. After we've talked to Marsh I want to call on your parents.'

'Why? If you're planning to tell them about what I've been up to, forget it. They won't be too worried. They're used to my antics. They're reconciled to the fact that it comes under the heading of research.'

'That's not why I want to talk to them. I was planning to ask them if I can marry you.'

Her eyes shone.

'You don't have to ask them. The answer's yes, yes, a thousand times yes. How soon can we get married?'

Her enthusiasm touched and stirred Dan. He lifted her determined little chin with his finger and kissed her in the middle of the busy road.

'Someone has to take you in hand to save you from yourself, and now that's settled, our first priority is to speak to Marsh.'

Back in the office, he reached for his phone, dialled Marsh's number and between them relayed Kate's latest information to the inspector.

'It's not much to go on,' Marsh said.

'But you will follow it up?' Dan pressed.

He hoped Kate couldn't hear what amounted to a tired sigh and the words, 'We'll look into it.'

'I'd think I'd make a better detective than him,' Kate said pouting, after Dan hung up. 'Another forty-eight hours and I'd have found out what Brian Porter is playing at.'

'Kate,' he said, 'you promised to let it go and I expect you to do just that.'

She laughed. 'Mr Kingston, I do believe you're already playing the head of the house,' she teased.

'Next stop, your parents. Call me old-fashioned, but I want to ask their permission to marry you,' Dan said.

How typical of him, how delightfully old-fashioned! And how she loved him for it.

'OK,' she said, her eyes shining, 'but the way they feel about you, I think they'd pay you to become their son-in-law.'

At the Drewett house, Kate began by asking her parents to sit down because they were in for a shock.

'Oh, dear, Kate, what have you been up to now?' Mrs Drewett complained.

'Nothing you won't approve of,' she said, attempting a wide-eyed, innocent look, 'but I thought you should know Dan has a new lady in his life.'

Her heart gave a hop, skip and jump. She was still getting used to being that lady. They'd discovered they loved one another in such a rush, and being with Dan had exceeded all her expectations, eclipsed any words she found for the emotions which swept over her whenever they were together. Would he always love her as he did today?

9

Dan couldn't remember ever being so happy, so content. They planned the wedding for the spring, and in deference to Kate, who wanted her literary friends there, and her parents, who wanted all the Drewett relations, he'd agreed to an all-the-trimmings affair.

He had six weeks to wait before he and Kate started their lives together; six weeks until he really belonged with her and shared everything with his sweet, impulsive Kate. Only her experiences with the crank caller continued to trouble him for Marsh hadn't come back to him with any answers.

He shrugged. In the last few days, there'd been no further contact or phone calls from Jonesy and no new developments. It was good news, but while the thing remained unresolved, he knew it would continue to needle Kate and test her patience. He picked up the phone.

'Marsh,' he said firmly, 'what progress have you made on the Porter business?'

'We've talked to the Toorak couple and to Rawlings and we have our suspicions, mate, but the Porters are well-known in high-up circles and big donors to the party in government at the moment. We have to tread carefully, and while the little lady believes Mr Porter is this Jonesy bloke, we don't have anything to suggest he's committed an offence.'

'What about public nuisance? Kate is willing to swear on oath that he's the man who posed as Jonesy.'

'You're a lawyer. You know as well as I do, we'd be wasting our time. It wouldn't stand up in court. Rawlings is the key, if he'd talk, but so far he's only admitting to a contract arrangement with the Porter company to do courier work for them.'

'They run an importing business. Could drugs be involved?'

Dan could almost hear the shrug of Marsh's heavy shoulders.

'Could, but unless we can find another connection between Rawlings and Porter, the investigation isn't going anywhere.'

'So, you're no closer to finding out why Kate was involved?'

'She was in the news with her book. We can be fairly certain that's why someone chose to involve her in their little scheme. But we can't rule out it being a hoax. Say, Kingston, the grapevine tells me you're going to marry the little lady.'

His lusty laughter prompted Dan to distance the phone from his ear.

'What's so funny?'

'Reckon I had to tell you you'd fallen for her, mate.'

Dan smiled to himself.

'Reckon I knew it a long time before you met her, mate.'

'Anyway, don't worry about her. If she's right and Porter is the culprit, she's as safe as houses now we've questioned him. He knows we're on to something so he won't risk taking things any further.'

'She'd better be, and keep on it,' Dan growled into the phone as he hung up.

Almost immediately, his phone rang. It was Keith Poole, the property agent for Normandy House.

'I'm wondering if you've confirmed your decision to buy the Molesworth place, sir? Your wife promised to get back to them within the hour and that was two hours ago. You can imagine how keen the old people are to sell to you. Mrs Molesworth is convinced you're the right people to live in their house. She really warmed to your wife.'

It took a few seconds for Dan to take in what he'd just heard.

'Excuse me? You've been talking to Ms Drew . . . I mean . . . my wife? When?'

'Not me. It's Mrs Molesworth. They spoke earlier today.'

Dan groaned, before hanging up with a gruff, 'Sorry, but I'll have to get back to you. We have an emergency here at the moment.'

★   ★   ★

Excited, Kate couldn't concentrate on writing, but it wasn't only excitement which stirred her. She hadn't worked out yet how to tell Dan her latest news. She started as someone knocked with urgency on the door of Writer's Cramp. Clearly it wasn't a casual visitor. It could only be Dan. Her heart went on hold. She knew this moment would come, but she'd hoped it would be in her own time.

'Katy Drewett, if you're trying to pretend you're not there, forget it. Open up.'

Though he kept his voice down, he sounded mildly threatening. Dan had obviously found out she'd been talking to the Molesworths, and as she expected, he wasn't pleased. But that would change once he learned what she'd discovered. Swinging open the door, she deliberately fell into his arms with a wide smile.

'Darling, what a lovely surprise.'

He held her firmly by the shoulders, hurried her inside, and closed the door.

'After all your promises, you've done it again, haven't you?'

She shrugged from his grasp, flopped into her chair.

'I hope we're not going to have the same old conversation again.'

'You promised me you'd leave everything to the police,' he said, his tone fiery.

'I don't think I promised that. I agreed to tell Marsh everything I knew.'

'And to leave it to him.'

'If you say so, but that was two days ago and nothing's happened. Anyway I don't know why you're making so much fuss. I can't get into trouble making phone calls.'

Dan looked down at her, frustrated.

'You're saying you didn't go out to the Molesworth home?'

'Of course not. You'd have done a big

wobbly if I'd gone anywhere near the Porter house.'

'When I thought you'd gone back to the Porter house I saw red.'

'You were worried about me?'

She stood up, went to his side, reached up and gave him a kiss. He reached out to her, held her close.

'Katy, love, I worry about you. I wish you weren't so impulsive.'

She ran the soft pad of her finger down his cheek, concern in her eyes.

'This isn't going to make any difference to us, is it? You still want me in your life?'

He kissed her before he murmured into her hair, 'My irresistible love, I'm not asking you to change. I fell in love with you as you are.'

'I sense there's a but somewhere in there,' she said, her sparkling eyes looking up to him.

With the touch of his finger under her chin he lifted her face.

'Nothing escapes you, does it? The but is, I want you to think of us as a partnership. I don't want you going off on your own without telling me first.'

'And I won't,' she promised.

She meant it, of course, but somehow he thought there would be times when her curiosity, her zest for life would win out, and he would learn to live with it.

'Hey,' she said, affirming how right his thought was, 'I'm bubbling over with news. You won't believe what I found out when I spoke to Mrs Molesworth.'

'I can wait until we go along to my office. I'm feeling a tad claustrophobic in here.'

'Good. Now you know what I want for a wedding present.'

He laughed as his arm slipped about her and they strolled along to his office. Inside, kissing her lightly, he lifted her to the corner of his desk, took his chair, and said, 'So what's your news? I can listen and admire your legs at the same time.'

She smirked.

'You'll find what I have to tell you far

more interesting than my legs. Stand by for the big production.'

'I'm on tenterhooks. What did Mrs Molesworth have to say?'

'You'll never guess who called at the Porter home several times recently at night — Drew Rawlings! Startling, isn't it?'

He raised interested brows.

'What evidence do you have to prove it was Rawlings?'

'The old lady saw . . . '

'Old ladies often have poor eyesight,' he broke in.

'She heard the motorbike, saw him park it discreetly around the back of the house and disappear inside.'

She took a deep breath.

'And she heard them arguing outside by the pool on a couple of occasions. The name Rawlings was mentioned. She said it sounded awful. Aren't I clever?'

Her smiling lips teased him.

'How does she know what Rawlings looks like?'

'I showed her a picture of him from a newspaper cutting.'

'I can't believe she heard and saw all that at night.'

'I told you, the poor, lonely old thing's pastime is curtain-peeping. Besides, the pool lights were on.'

'You're incredibly nosey. How did you get her to tell you all this?'

'With the truth. I simply said I was a writer, researching for a murder mystery. It fascinated her and she wanted to know all about it. We started chatting and . . . '

'In your usual persuasive manner she opened up to you.'

'Yes, but only after I agreed not to let the colonel know what she'd been saying. He doesn't want people to think unsavoury things go on in their area. She's such a sweet old darling, I've promised to call in and give her an autographed copy of my novel.'

'Very nice,' he muttered, as he picked up the phone and tapped out Marsh's number then passed Kate the receiver.

'But,' she wailed, after she'd spoken to Marsh, 'I won't have the chance to follow this up.'

'Don't tell me you've forgotten you have a wedding to plan and a deadline to meet on your next book.'

'I don't know why I tell you everything.'

'I do.' He grinned. 'It's because you love me.'

On the afternoon of the next day, Gary Marsh called at Dan's practice.

'We've made some headway on the crank caller thing. I thought you and the little lady would want to know.'

'Should we feel hopeful?' Dan asked as he phoned through to Writer's Cramp and invited Kate to join them.

'I think so,' Marsh replied.

'Good. Can I give you some advice? The little lady doesn't like being called that. She'd prefer Kate,' he said.

Marsh smiled.

Kate had one of her good feelings, and as she strolled into Dan's office, and was greeted as Kate by Marsh, she knew he was in agreement with her intuition. He sat wedged into a chair on the other side of Dan's desk as if he'd been planted there, his hands interlocked, his thumbs circling impatiently. She took the chair next to his.

'What's happened, Inspector?' she asked.

'A few hours ago, we arrested Drew Rawlings for blackmail. He was about to leave town when we picked him up. Your latest piece of information came in very handy, Miss Drewett.'

Kate's mouth almost flew open.

'Rawlings? Blackmail? Whom was he blackmailing?'

'The Porters. He was persuaded to make a full confession and to implicate them after we hinted we had a witness to an unpleasant confrontation he had with him.'

'And what did he have on the Porters? No, don't tell me.' Her mind was on the move. 'He'd threatened to shop them to the police when he discovered he was couriering around illegal drugs for them.'

'You knew?' Dan asked, leaning forward.

'No, but it's the only thing that makes sense. What I still haven't worked out is why the elaborate plan involving me? I know Brian Porter acted as Jonesy, and I think we can assume that it was he and his stuck-up wife who took you on that motorbike chase in and out of the pubs, after he left me at the Northland carpark, Dan.' She shrugged, gestured with her hands. 'But why were the Porters so anxious for me to report Helen Porter's life was in danger? What was that all about?'

'We've got some idea. How would you feel about coming out to the Porter home and surprising them?'

Dan stood up, raised his palms.

'No, Gary, it's not going to happen. Kate's done enough of your work for you. You're on your own from here,' he said firmly.

She went to his side, looked up at him.

'Dearest Dan, I want to do this. I want to file the Porter affair away before our wedding. After we marry, you'll have lots of opportunities to speak up for me.'

'Is that what I was doing?'

'Yes, mate, it was, and today's lively young women don't take too kindly to it. Reckon it's time Kate took you in hand.' Marsh had a huge grin on his face. 'She'll be safe as houses.'

'You'd better believe it because I'm coming, too.'

* * *

Marsh led a group of police officers, two in uniform, up the pebbled drive of the Porter home, and ordered one of them to press the button. When Helen Porter came to the door, she raised pencilled eyebrows, gave them a patronising stare and said, 'This is the second time you've come here to pester us, so make it the last, or we'll lodge a complaint of harassment.'

'Can we come in?' Marsh said harshly.

'If you must.'

They were shown into a large home office where Brian Porter sat at a computer. He turned sharply, exchanged glances with his wife and, standing up, demanded, 'What is it this time?'

Then he spotted Dan and Kate, wearing the charity clothes of their first visit to the home.

'What the devil is this all about? What are those two religious cranks doing back here?'

'They're not trying to save you, quite the opposite. Can I examine your right hand, sir?' Marsh asked.

Porter thrust his hand in the inspector's face. After examining it, Marsh said, 'Thank you, sir, for your co-operation.'

'Is that all?'

'Not quite. We have a warrant to search your offices and this home for drugs.'

That was Kate's cue to sweep off her

wig and glasses.

'I think we've met before, Mr Porter, when you masqueraded under the name of Tom Jones.'

Porter turned pale, his wife crossed to stand beside him and raised her head in a haughty gesture.

'Don't you dare say anything, Brian, until our solicitors arrive. They've got nothing on us.'

★   ★   ★

By arrangement, Kate and Dan met Inspector Marsh for a celebratory drink at the Drover's Dog Hotel. They sat in a comfortable nook, a quiet distance from the bar.

'I promised you a rundown of what happened after you left yesterday. But before I do so, let me thank you, Kate, for coming to the house. It well and truly unnerved the bloke. Anyway, we found a huge cache of drugs in the factory and the Porters are awaiting a bail application. As for Rawlings, poor soul, after discovering the Porters' little game, he threatened to blow the whistle on them if they didn't give him a piece of the action.'

'Ah, it's all falling into shape,' Kate said, nodding. 'My detective, Fabian Farley, would at that stage have the cold, greedy couple decided he had to go, and planning a murder.'

Marsh nodded.

'Go on, go on.'

'So they hatch an evil plan to . . . ' She stopped, shook her hands in frustration. 'I can't quite put the last few pieces together.'

'Brian Porter was easy to break down during questioning. He was more than anxious to put the blame on to his dear wife when he knew what sentences drug importers and traffickers can get. Apparently, involving you was her idea. The plan was to notify the police that Helen Porter's life was being threatened, and to lure Rawlings to the house and . . . '

'Got it!' Kate yelled with excitement.

Dan looked puzzled. 'I certainly haven't.'

'Allow me,' she said with a grin. 'The cold, confident Mrs Porter would accidentally shoot Rawlings at the house, and later claim he'd tried to assault her when she discovered him robbing the place. But the really devious part of the plot was to have the coppers believe a hitman had been engaged to murder her. That way, they'd accept her story and assume Rawlings was the hitman, and she'd plead accident, or self defence.'

Dan frowned. 'But wouldn't the husband come under suspicion?'

Kate's smirk returned. 'Naturally, he'd have a watertight alibi.'

Dan smiled. 'Now why didn't I think of that?'

'Because you haven't got my enquiring mind. Have you worked out why they tried to involve me, yet?'

He nodded. 'You were the key to the plan. It all hinged on you informing the police Mrs Porter's life was in danger.'

Marsh shifted his considerable bulk on the padded bench.

'Did I mention she attended one of your book launches? We found a signed copy of your novel and a magazine featuring the real-life hitman's story in a bundle of old papers in Mrs Porter's office, and a motorbike with false registration plates under wraps in one of their garages.'

'Why on earth would they leave that lying around?' Kate asked.

'They thought they might need it again.'

Dan held up his glass to Kate.

'To you, my impulsive, headstrong, persistent girl. The Porters supposed that a twenty-two-year-old crime writer would swallow the story and go running to the police. If they'd asked me, I'd have told them they chose to manipulate the wrong woman. You'd never have done what they wanted without first trying to find out what it was all about.'

'To the little lady.' Marsh raised his glass.

'And to Mrs Molesworth,' Kate added. 'Rawlings could be dead if it hadn't been for her information.'

Marsh shook his head. 'They'd never have risked it unless you played your part, Kate. Rawlings is alive today because of your curiosity.'

She smiled, looked up at Dan.

'Are you listening, Daniel, darling? The inspector thinks I did good.'

Dan moved closer to her, stole a quick kiss.

'You've had your fun. It's time to settle down to a quiet life now.'

'I still have a few weeks to kick up my heels before I become an old married lady.'

'Ahem,' Marsh interrupted. 'A bloke better get home before he's accused of being a gooseberry. Thanks, Kate,' he added as he hauled himself from the padded bench.

⋆ ⋆ ⋆

'That was beautiful, Mrs Drewett. You deserve a medal for your roasts,' Dan said, as they sat around the dinner table on the eve of the wedding.

Mrs Drewett beamed. 'Anyone can cook a roast.'

'Not like you.'

'I could give Kate a few lessons.'

'Don't even think about it, Mum. Writers don't have time.'

Dan smiled indulgently at his fiancée before shrugging.

'You'd probably be wasting your time anyway, Mrs Drewett. Your daughter would get diverted plotting a story about a sheep-station murder, or how to place undetected poison into mint sauce and burn the dinner.'

They all laughed.

'Don't worry, though. Mum and Dad will expect us for dinner regularly. You can get your fix of roasts, then.'

'Any time, Dan, and I'm hoping we might get some golf or fishing in at the weekends,' Mr Drewett added.

'You're going to have to drink an

awful lot of Mum's camomile tea and eat her bran muffins, too. It's what you have to expect when you belong to this family,' she whispered, pressing her lips to his.

Dan couldn't wait to belong to this family — to his beloved Kate.

The End